way, I never thought it was, but making posters turned out to be one of the easiest parts of running for office. The hardest part was how I had to go around being nice to people all the time. And how I had to always keep smiling. I'm not kidding. I even had to smile at kids who make me sick.

Maxie said it's called "sucking up." He said it's the American way.

Kids love Barbara Park's books so much, they've given them all these awards:

Alabama's Emphasis on Reading

Arizona Young Readers' Award

Charlotte Award (New York State)

Dorothy Canfield Fisher Children's Book Award (Vermont)

Flicker Tale Children's Book Award (North Dakota)

Georgia Children's Book Award

Golden Archer Award (Wisconsin)

Great Stone Face Award (New Hampshire)

Iowa Children's Choice Award

IRA-CBC Children's Choice

IRA Young Adults' Choice

Junior Book Award (South Carolina)

Library of Congress Book of the Year

Maud Hart Lovelace Award (Minnesota)

Milner Award (Georgia)

Nevada Young Readers' Award

North Dakota Children's Choice Award

Nutmeg Children's Book Award (Connecticut)

OMAR Award (Indiana)

Parents' Choice Award

Rebecca Caudill Young Readers' Book Award (Illinois)

Rhode Island Children's Book Award

Sasquatch Reading Award of Washington State

School Library Journal's Best Children's Book of the Year

Tennessee Children's Choice Book Award

Texas Bluebonnet Award

Utah Children's Book Award

West Virginia Honor Book

William Allen White Children's Book Award (Kansas)

Young Hoosier Book Award (Indiana)

BOOKS BY BARBARA PARK:

The GEEK CHRONICLES 2

Rosie Swanson: Fourth-Grade Geek for President

Barbara Park

Random House New York

To the special man I get to call my dad…
Happy eighty-fifth birthday!
—B.P.

A RANDOM HOUSE BOOK
Text copyright © 1991 by Barbara Park
Cover art copyright © 2000 by Peter Van Ryzin

All rights reserved under International and Pan-American Copyright
Conventions. Published in the United States by Random House, Inc.,
New York, and simultaneously in Canada by Random House of Canada
Limited, Toronto. Originally published in hardcover as a Borzoi Book by
Alfred A. Knopf, Inc., in 1991.

www.randomhouse.com/kids

Library of Congress Catalog Card Number: 91-8616
ISBN: 0-679-83371-4
RL: 4.3

Printed in the United States of America
September 2000
10 9 8 7 6 5 4 3

RANDOM HOUSE and colophon are registered trademarks of Random House, Inc.

* CONTENTS *

THE GEEK CHRONICLES 2:

Rosie Swanson: Fourth-Grade Geek for President

1 ROSIE SWANSON— SECRET INFORMER

"HEY, YOU! NERDHEADS! GET OFF THE SWINGS!"

The voice came from behind us.

Maxie and Earl and I spun around. Three sixth-grade boys were hurrying toward us.

"YEAH, *YOU* THREE!" the kid shouted again. "THE FAT KID, THE SKINNY KID, AND THE FOUR-EYED, GEEKY GIRL! IS SOMETHING WRONG WITH YOUR EARS, DUDES? I SAID, GET OFF THE SWINGS! IT'S OUR TURN."

Earl jumped right up. Since Earl Wilber is a little on the plumpish side, he always likes to get a head start when he's making a break for it. "No, wait, Earl! Don't run," I said quickly. "If we run, they'll just chase us. Let's stay right where we are and pretend we didn't hear them."

Nervously, Earl sat back down. Even though

he and Maxie are in fifth grade and I'm only in fourth, they still listen to me sometimes.

I hunched over and tried to pull my head inside my turtleneck sweater. Everything fit except my glasses.

Maxie's eyes were squeezed shut. "We're dead people," he muttered. For some reason, he started to spell it. "D-E-A-D P-E-O-P—"

"No, we're not," I snapped. "We're not going to die, Maxie. Who ever heard of dying on a swing set?"

Maxie opened one eye and looked at me. "News flash. Little people die wherever big people kill them. It's a law of physics. Look it up."

By now, the sixth-graders were right behind us. Angry that we still hadn't moved, they grabbed the chains of our swings and began shaking them.

"You guys don't hear too good, do you?" said the biggest one.

Earl started to whimper a little. I was scared, too. But something inside me just wouldn't let me give the kid my swing.

"We were here first," I managed.

The three bullies bent down and laughed in

my face. *"We were here first, we were here first,"* they mimicked in baby voices.

After that, the big one leaned right next to my ear. "GET OFF, GIRLIE!"

I don't like to be shouted at. Also, I hate being called a girlie.

"No!" I said back. "These are our swings, too, you know."

Hearing myself say that made me feel a little braver. "If you don't leave us alone, I'm going to report you to the principal," I said.

Suddenly, the kid jerked my swing so hard I thought my head would snap off.

"Gee, girlie. I'm shaking in my shoes. Aren't you, Frankie? Aren't you shaking in your shoes?" he asked his friend.

After that, the three of them started twisting our chains around and around until our swings were all wound up in little knots. We were way off the ground.

"We don't care that you're doing this, you know," I said. "We actually like this. This is fun. We love being twisted, in fact."

The bullies stopped twisting.

"ONE…TWO…THREE!" they hollered.

On "three," they grabbed our swing seats and spun us as hard as they could.

"Bye-bye, you little dipsticks!" they called as they ran off.

I've never twirled so fast in my life. Not even on that carnival ride where everyone throws up.

Next to me, Earl was making a high-pitched whining sound—like a siren, sort of. Earl is one of those kids who has to keep nose drops in his pocket to clear out his sinuses. Also, he has a mouth inhaler. But if he needed it now, there was no way he could get it while he was spinning.

Maxie said a bad word. It was only one syllable, but he dragged it out for the entire time he was untwisting.

It took forever for us to unwind. I mean it. It seemed like we would spin for years. But even after our swings stopped, none of us got up right away. We just laid our heads on our knees and moaned for a while until the world stopped moving so fast.

Finally, I held on to the chain with one hand and stood up. I tried to smooth out my dress without falling over.

"There. See? That wasn't so bad, was it?" I asked.

The two of them moaned some more.

"I don't care. We did the right thing by not running," I said. "Bullies like that make me sick. They don't own the school, you know. Sometimes kids like us just have to stand up for our rights."

Maxie raised his head. His eyes looked like cartoon eyes—all round and white, with a little black dot in the middle.

Earl was holding his hand over his mouth, trying not to throw up.

"Okay, okay. I know it wasn't fun," I said. "But at least we didn't give in. We're just as much a part of this school as anybody else. And it's time we acted like it."

Slowly, Maxie got off the swing. He helped Earl stand up. Then they both fell over in the grass.

I still can't believe I'm best friends with these two. But I am.

I gave them each a hand. "Come on, you guys. We need to go report those creeps to the principal's office before the bell rings."

Earl shook his head. "Oh no. No way, Rosie. Forget it. I'm not squealing. And besides, I'm never setting foot in the principal's office again. I still get nightmares about the last time we were all in there. *Real* nightmares, I mean. The kind where I wake up all tangled in the sheets and I have to turn on the light."

"I agree," said Maxie. "If Mr. Shivers gets to know the three of us any better, we'll be on his Christmas list."

I just sighed. I hated to admit it, but I knew they were right. It wasn't even November yet, and each of us had been to the office two times already. Actually, it's where we first met.

I was sent for passing notes. I wasn't passing them to the other kids, though. I was passing them to my teacher, Mr. Jolly. None of my classmates knows this about me, but in my head, I picture myself as Rosie Swanson—Secret Informer. I report on rule breakers. I think of it as my job, sort of.

Even Maxie and Earl don't know I'm a secret informer. I mean, they know I'm a nut about following school rules and everything. Like I always make them cross at the crosswalks, for instance. But I've never told them about the note writing and how I tell on people. I know they'd think I'm a tattletale. And I'm not.

Secret informers are different from tattletales. We don't tell on other kids just to get them in trouble. We do it for their own good. Reporting illegal activities to your teacher helps bad kids understand that they can't get away with stuff, and they become better citizens.

I've been a secret informer since the summer I turned seven. That's the summer my mother and I went into a candy store at the beach and I spotted an old lady stealing a piece of saltwater taffy. She took it out of one of the jars, unwrapped it, and popped it right into her mouth without paying for it.

I couldn't believe it! I'm talking about a *grandma* here. Except for when they drive, you almost never see grandmas break the law.

I still remember how I stopped what I was doing and watched her chew. Only instead of being embarrassed, she winked at me. You know...like we were both in on this together.

I've thought about it a lot since then. And I've decided that winking was even worse than taking the candy. Because that old lady tried to make a little girl think it was okay to steal. And that was just wrong, you know? It was just plain wrong.

I still get angry about it. Since then, I've taught myself to say "The old lady took a taffy" without moving my lips, but I doubt that I'll ever get to use it.

Anyway, after that happened, I decided that I was never going to just stand around while somebody broke the law again. So that's when I became a secret informer.

I've had a lot of success with spying over the years. Take Ronald Milligan, for instance. Since I wrote a secret note to my teacher, Ronald has been asked to stop blowing his nose in the drinking fountain. I take a lot of pride in that.

But still, for some reason, my teacher, Mr. Jolly, hasn't really appreciated my spying as much as you'd expect. Like I mentioned, that's why he finally sent me to the principal's office. To get me to stop writing notes. And the office is where I met Maxie and Earl.

As I was remembering all of this, Earl reached in his pocket and unwrapped a brand-new package of Rolaids. In addition to his other medical problems, Earl Wilber has what you call a nervous stomach.

"I wish I ran this school," he said. "If I ran this school, I'd lock those sixth-grade creeps in a dark, smelly dungeon. Then I'd hire one of those professional wrestler guys to bully them until they cried."

Maxie nodded. "I know just how you feel," he said. "But Rosie's probably right, Earl. We shouldn't let farkleberries like that get to us."

Farkleberry is one of Maxie's special words. Finding weird words in the dictionary is sort of a hobby of his. That's because he's a giant brain.

Maxie's very different from Earl and me. But even though the three of us aren't anything alike—if you put us all together, we'd make a pretty well-rounded person, I think.

Earl was still grouching. "Yeah, well, I still wish I could run the school. They're having those stupid class elections pretty soon, and the same popular kids will get elected who always get elected. And not one of them knows the least bit about how it feels to be called names and pushed around."

"Run," said Maxie.

Suddenly, Earl's face went funny. "Oh geez! Not again!" he yelled. Then, thinking the bullies were back, he took off across the playground.

Maxie rolled his eyes. "No, Earl! Come back!" he hollered after him. "I meant run for *office*."

Earl stopped in his tracks. "Oh," he said, embarrassed.

He turned around and came back. "Yeah, right. Me...president of the fifth grade," he said. "Very funny, Mr. Funnyperson. That's so funny I forgot to laugh."

Maxie shrugged. "Well, you're always complaining about the creeps around here, aren't you? So maybe if you ran for president of the fifth grade, you could change some stuff."

I thought about what he was saying. I mean, it's just weird, you know? But the idea that one of us could actually run for class office had never even occurred to me before.

"What about me?" I said. "I bet I'd make a

pretty good fourth-grade president, don't you think? Huh, you guys? Don't you think I'd be good?"

Maxie and Earl gave each other one of those *looks.*

"What did you do that for? What's wrong with me being president of the fourth grade?" I asked.

Earl shrugged. "Nothing's exactly *wrong* with it, Rosie," he said. "It's just that sometimes you can be a little bit…"

He hemmed and hawed. "Well, you know…"

"Bossy and overbearing," said Max.

"I am not," I snapped. "I'm not bossy and whatever that other word means. I just happen to believe in following the rules, that's all. What's so wrong with that? In case you've forgotten, my grandfather happens to be a retired police detective."

Maxie's mouth dropped open. "No! Really? You're kidding! Gee, I think that's only the jillionth time you've told us that. Isn't it, Earl? Isn't that the jillionth?"

Earl pretended to count on his fingers. Then he shook his head. "The jillionth and one," he said.

They were only teasing, but it still hurt my feelings. I'm very proud of my grandfather. He's part of the reason I'm such a model citizen.

He and my mother and I all live in the same house that Mom grew up in. It's just the three of us, too. We're sort of a different kind of family, I guess you'd say. We would have been a regular kind of family, but my father and my grandmom both died when I was a baby.

I don't have any brothers or sisters. I used to have a girlfriend who was almost like a sister. But we haven't spoken in over a year. It wasn't my fault, exactly. She spray-painted a bad word on the sidewalk and I was forced to report her to the police.

Anyhow, even though my granddad is retired, he still hangs around the police station a lot. Sometimes when I go down there with him, this one sergeant lets me wear his hat. I've met criminals down there before, too. Not the real dangerous kind. But still, most of them haven't shaved for a while.

"It's not very nice calling me bossy, you know," I told Maxie. "And anyway, I don't care what you say, I still think I'd make a good class president. I have excellent values and I follow the rules. Plus also, I have a bullhorn, which I could bring to school to keep the children in order."

Maxie raised his eyebrows. "Are you serious?" he asked. "You have a real, actual bullhorn? An official one? Like the cops use on TV?"

"Yup," I said. "It's my grandfather's, but I've used it before. Just ask my mother if you don't believe me. Last summer I snuck outside with it. And I ordered her to come out of the house with her hands up."

Now Earl was impressed, too. "Wow! And she *did* it? She really raised her hands and came outside?"

"Well, kind of," I said. "I mean, at first she just went to the window and yelled at me to put it down. But then some of the neighbors who were out in their yards started chanting, 'Come out, Helen! Come out!' So finally she ran outside and snatched the bullhorn away from me."

"Wow," said Earl, again.

"Yeah, wow," I agreed. "A bullhorn is a pretty powerful piece of equipment, all right."

I didn't tell them the best part about that day, though. It would have sounded stupid to say it. But the best part of that day was how that bullhorn turned a little voice like mine into a loud, booming voice that everyone listened to.

A voice of *authority*, I guess you'd say.

And I'm telling you the truth...a voice of authority can make you feel bigger than anything.

2 TO RUN OR NOT TO RUN?

ROSEBUD SWANSON FOR PRESIDENT OF THE FOURTH GRADE

The idea kept flashing on and off in my head like a neon sign. I'm not kidding. Ever since I mentioned it on the playground, I couldn't get it out of my mind.

ROSEBUD SWANSON FOR PRESIDENT OF THE FOURTH GRADE

Boy. That'd show everyone, wouldn't it? If I was president of the whole entire fourth grade, I bet Maxie and Earl and I would never get picked on again.

The idea wasn't totally impossible, you know. I mean, you don't *have* to be cute or popular to run for president. It's not an actual requirement or anything.

At school we have a poster of the presidents of the United States, and practically none of those guys were cute. George Washington even had weird-looking hair. I realize that weird-looking hair was in style back then, but I still think one of his friends should have pulled him over and said, "Hey, George. Change the 'do.'"

Anyway, maybe it was just a coincidence, but at the exact same time the thoughts about becoming president were floating around in my head, my teacher read an announcement about the class election.

"There's going to be a candidates' meeting for fourth-graders right after school," he read from the school bulletin. "Anyone who is interested in running for class office should report to room thirteen—that's Mrs. Munson's room—at three o'clock sharp."

As soon as he said it, I got butterflies in my stomach and goose bumps came on my arms. The kind of goose bumps that don't go away when you rub them.

"That's today, right, sir?" I called out. "The meeting's today?"

A couple of kids turned around and looked at me. They rolled their eyes as if they couldn't believe a person like me would even *think* about running.

Judith Topper, the jerky girl who sits right in front of me, was one of them. The two of us aren't that fond of each other.

"Yeah, right, Rosie," she said. "Like you could really win an election. You're not cute. And you're not popular. Get a clue, okay?"

"Oh really, Judith?" I said back. "Well, if I'm not cute, then what does that make you? Repulsive or putrid? Pick one."

Judith made a face at me. "Geek," she said.

That's when I really started to boil inside. It's just not fair, that's all. Why does being cute and popular have to be so important? Why isn't it ever enough just to be a regular, average person?

There're lots of us around, you know. In fact, almost everybody in my entire class is just a regular, average person. Some of them even wear glasses like I do.

Also, there are kids with crooked teeth and braces and dumb haircuts and big noses and ears that stick out. We even have two boys in our room who can put you to sleep just by talking to you.

I felt myself relax a little. *Average*. It's not a bad word, really. It's nice, in fact. Comfortable, sort of.

Norman Beeman caught me looking at him and blushed. Norman is one of the dumb haircuts. Also, he has fat, freckled fingers. And sometimes he wears yellow fishing boots to school. I would like to ask him about the boots, but Norman Beeman scares me a little.

He'd probably vote for me, though. Norman Beeman would probably love to vote for a person who wasn't perfect or popular. I bet lots of kids would.

The more I thought about it, the better I felt about my chances. I mean, I was still really nervous about going to the meeting and all. But I was beginning to think that I really might give it a try.

Just then, Mr. Jolly told us to get out our history books. I looked down at some of the presidents pictured on the cover. For the most part, it was not an attractive group.

I closed my eyes and tried to imagine what it would feel like to win a school election. I pictured myself standing on the school stage giving a victory speech. I was holding my bullhorn and there was a giant American flag hanging behind me. I was thanking all the average kids who voted for me. Then I thanked the below-average ones, too. After that, I found Judith Topper in the crowd and I had a security guard drag her to detention.

Three o'clock came fast that day. When the bell rang, my heart was pounding faster than ever. I grabbed my backpack and ran straight to the girls' bathroom. When you're really, really excited about getting to a meeting, the worst thing you can do is be the first one there. It makes you look totally desperate.

I stood at the sink and washed my hands for a while. If you dry each finger with a separate paper towel, you can use up a lot of time. I would have been there longer, but Mrs. Galonka, the head custodian, saw all the towels I was using and started yelling, "Whoa, whoa, whoa!"

When I finally left the girls' room, I walked as

slowly as I could to room 13. Then I took a deep breath and went inside.

Mrs. Munson and Mr. Jolly were standing in the front of the room. There are four fourth-grade teachers at Dooley Elementary. But since Mr. Jolly and Mrs. Munson have been there the longest, they're almost always the bosses.

Mr. Jolly smiled at me. "Rosie Swanson! Good. I was beginning to think that no one from my class was going to show up."

Mrs. Munson went to the door and looked up and down the hall. "Are you the last of the stragglers?" she asked.

I didn't appreciate being called a straggler, but I didn't say anything. Instead, I went straight to the back of the room and sat down. The other kids were sitting nearer the front. I knew almost all of them.

Nic and Vic Timmerman were right in front of Mrs. Munson's desk. In case you haven't guessed it, Nic and Vic are twins. The weird kind of twins, I mean. The kind who don't understand that they're actually two separate people. Like if you call one of them, they both come. In first grade, when Nic broke his arm, Vic wore a sling. Also, they finished each other's sentences, just like Huey, Dewey, and Louie.

One seat over from the Timmerman twins was this really cute girl named Summer Lynne Jones. That's her real name, too. Summer Lynne. It must be nice to have a mother who doesn't feel it's necessary to name you after her dead Aunt Rosebud.

Two desks behind Summer Lynne Jones was this boy I went to kindergarten with. His name is Alan Allen. I'd like to make fun of it, but I have an uncle named Harry Harry. And besides, when you're the best soccer player in the fourth grade, and you look almost exactly like Michael Jordan, your name could be Piggly Wiggly and no one would care. They'd just pat you on the back, say "Good game, Piggly," and that would be that.

A girl named Louise the Disease was sitting next to the window. That's not her real name, but she always has a cold, so that's what everyone calls her. She deliberately sneezed on me in assembly last year. I reported her to the nurse, but no action was taken.

Roxanne Handleman was right behind Louise the Disease. I used to know Roxanne, but I don't anymore. One time when we were in kindergarten, she came over to my house to play. She wore a nurse's outfit and made me call her Florence. It was the longest afternoon of my life.

Next to Roxanne was this girl named Karla something, who I didn't know much about. Then there were three kids from Mrs. Munson's class. I didn't know them, either, but they were acting really cool—like they were the "in crowd," or something—so I decided not to like them.

Mr. Jolly grabbed a piece of chalk and walked over to the board. "Okay, let's get started. I want to welcome everyone to our meeting this afternoon and tell you how glad Mrs. Munson and I are that so many of you have decided to run for class office."

He took his chalk and wrote the words "President," "Vice President," "Secretary," and "Treasurer." Underneath each title he left room for names.

"The first thing we need to do is find out which office each of you wants to run for," he said.

"Let's begin with president, okay? How many of you came here today to run for president of the fourth grade? Let's see your hands."

My heart started to pound again. I closed my eyes and secretly prayed that I would be the only one. When I opened them, Nic and Vic Timmerman were waving their hands all over the place.

Mr. Jolly looked puzzled. "Wait a second. You mean you *both* want to run for president? Do you really think that's a good idea, guys? For two brothers to run *against* each other?"

The Timmerman twins shook their heads. "We don't want to run *against* each other, Mr. Jolly," said Vic. "We want to run *together*. As a team. You know, the fourth grade will get two presidents—"

"—for the price of one," finished Nic.

Mrs. Munson didn't waste a second. "Oh no. No way," she said flatly. "Absolutely not, gentlemen."

Nic and Vic looked shocked.

"But why not?" asked Vic.

"Yeah, how come?" asked Nic. "It'd be perfect. We could do twice as much work as one

23

president. And if one of us got sick, the other one could—"

"—take his place," finished Vic. "It'd be—"

"—perfect," said Nic.

Mrs. Munson crossed her arms. "I'm sorry, boys, but class president is not tag-team wrestling. We're trying to teach you something about government. And in our government, there's only one president. You two think it over, and we'll get back to you in a few minutes."

The Timmermans put their heads down on their desks.

Mrs. Munson moved along. "Okay, who else wants to run for president?"

I took a deep breath and started to raise my hand. That's when Alan Allen's arm shot into the air.

"Me! I do," he said.

Then Summer Lynne Jones raised her hand, too. She fluttered her fingers and waved to get Mr. Jolly's attention.

My insides went limp. Seriously. It was like somebody let all my air out. All this time, I had just been kidding myself about being able to win an election. Why would anyone vote for regular, average *me,* when they could vote for cute and popular *them?*

Mr. Jolly searched the room for more volunteers. I sat on my hands and slumped down in my seat.

Finally, he moved on. "Okay then. How about vice president? Who came here today to run for VP?"

Both of the girls from Mrs. Munson's room called out their names. Then they looked at each other and crossed their fingers. I wondered if they would still be so buddy-buddy after the election.

When Mr. Jolly got to class secretary, Karla something and Roxanne Handleman both started waving. Roxanne tried to raise her hand the highest. Seeing this, Karla something got on her knees and stretched even taller. Finally, Roxanne stood on her chair.

Watching them made me embarrassed to be a girl.

Next came treasurer. Louise the Disease raised her Kleenex over her head. "Louise Marie Smythe!" she yelled.

As soon as she said it, the boy from Mrs. Munson's class cupped his hands around his mouth and shouted, "Robert Moneypenny! Robert Moneypenny for treasurer!"

Louise the Disease stared at him in disbelief. "That's your *real* name? Your real name is Robert Moneypenny?"

The boy grinned and leaned his chair back on two legs.

Louise the Disease frowned. "But that's not fair! Is that fair? His name is too good. It gives him an advantage."

When Mrs. Munson said it was fair, Louise the Disease turned to Robert Moneypenny and coughed on him.

After that, there were only three of us left. Nic and Vic and me.

Mr. Jolly went back to the twins. "Have you two gentlemen decided what you want to do yet?"

Nic and Vic looked at each other and began raising their eyebrows up and down. It's like they were talking in some creepy kind of "twin" language or something.

Finally, they looked up. "Treasurer and vice president," they said at the same time.

Mr. Jolly picked up his chalk. "Okay. Fine. Which one of you will be running for which job?"

Nic shrugged glumly. "Who cares? What difference—"

"—does it make?" said Vic.

They were still figuring it out when Mrs. Munson glanced in my direction.

"What about you in the back? What office are you interested in? We've got lots of other things to discuss and we're running out of time."

Everyone turned around. That's the bad thing about sitting in the back. Everybody always turns around.

I didn't know what to do. I mean, I've never, ever been a quitter before, but...

"Rosie, *please*," said Mr. Jolly. "We really need to know, okay? What office?"

I closed my eyes and bit my bottom lip.

"President," I heard myself say. "I guess I'm running for president."

3 ME AND THOMAS JEFFERSON

It was Saturday, and as usual, Maxie and Earl and I were hanging out in Maxie's garage. Maxie's father has an old 1955 red-and-white Chevy that the three of us use as a clubhouse, sort of. Mr. Zuckerman thinks he's going to fix it up someday. But Maxie says it'll probably rust in the garage for another twenty years, and then some guy with tattoos will come haul it to the dump for fifty bucks.

Anyhow, while we were sitting there, Earl and Maxie were having this stupid argument about whether dogs were better than cats. I wasn't joining in, though. I was still depressed about the candidates' meeting. And I'm not one of those people who can act all happy when I'm not. Besides that, their stupid cat-and-dog argument was turning so idiotic it was embarrassing just to listen to it.

Earl kept saying that stinky cats needed

stinky litter boxes. And Maxie kept arguing that bad-breath dogs drank from germy toilets.

Finally, I couldn't stand it anymore. "Yeah, well, guess what? I hate this whole stinky, germy conversation. So why don't you both just knock it off."

Maxie and Earl looked at me. They had been trying their best to ignore my bad mood. But I could have told them it wouldn't work. When I'm pouty, I am very persistent.

"Okay, fine," Maxie said. "I guess we might as well get this over with. What the heck's wrong with you this morning, anyway? Why are you acting like such a *dingle?*"

"I am *not* a dingle," I snapped. "It just so happens that I have a lot on my mind right now. And don't ask me what it is, either. Because I don't want to talk about it."

I waited for them to ask. But they didn't. That's the trouble with boys. When you tell them not to ask, they respect your wishes.

"All right, fine," I said finally. "I'll tell you. But when I'm finished telling you, I'm not going to talk about it."

I took a deep breath. "Okay, brace yourselves…

"I'm officially running for president of the fourth grade."

Maxie's mouth dropped open. "What?" he said.

"You're joking," said Earl.

"No, I'm not *joking*," I said back. "And I don't want to talk about it anymore. It makes me feel pukey inside."

Right away, Earl started rolling down the windows to give me fresh air. He takes "pukey" very seriously.

"I'm not *really* going to puke, Earl," I said. "If I was really going to puke, I would have done it by now. But you should hear who I'm running against. It'll make you guys sick, too."

I squeezed my eyes shut and said the names. "Summer Lynne Jones and Alan Allen."

I was hoping that when I opened my eyes again, Maxie and Earl would be looking puzzled…as if they'd never *heard* of Summer and Alan Allen. But when I finally peeked at him, Maxie seemed almost as sick as me.

"Oh man. Not good," he whispered.

"Not good?" said Earl. "Try *hopeless*."

He reached over and gave me a sympathetic pat. "I feel your pain," he said quietly.

For some reason, this comment made me totally annoyed at him.

"How, Earl?" I asked. "How can you feel my pain? Huh? Have you ever run for office against two of the most popular kids in the school?"

"Well, not exactly," he said. "In second grade, I nominated myself for Cub of the Month. But unfortunately, as soon as I did it, the den mother rolled her eyes and said, 'Get real, Earl.'"

Maxie couldn't believe it. "Are you serious? That's *terrible*, Earl. You told your mother, didn't you? At least, I hope you did."

Earl stared at his hands awhile before he answered. "The den mother *was* my mother," he said finally.

Maxie looked at him a minute. Then he totally cracked up. He doubled up into a little ball and started rolling all around the front seat.

"Not funny, not funny, not funny!" yelled Earl. But his yelling only made Maxie laugh harder.

Suddenly, I just wanted to go home. As I

opened the car door, Maxie's head appeared over the top of the seat. He had tears in his eyes from laughing so hard.

"Where're you going?" he asked, trying to get himself under control. "You're not leaving, are you? Come on, Rosie. Don't go. We've got to talk about this."

One of my feet was already on the garage floor. Maxie jumped out of the car and put it back inside. He closed the door again, then hopped back into the front seat.

"Listen to me, Rosie," he said. "It's *good* that you're running for president of your class. You're the one who's always talking about how we should stand up for ourselves, right? So, go for it. It's not as hopeless as you think. I swear. My father ran for town council last year, so I know a ton about campaigning."

That didn't really surprise me. Maxie knows a ton about everything.

"Your dad's on the town council?" asked Earl.

Maxie squirmed a little. "What does that have to do with anything, Earl? There are more important things in life than just winning, you know.

Winning, winning, winning—that's all anyone ever thinks about."

Earl looked at me. "He lost," he said.

"So what?" snapped Maxie. "He *could* have won. The only reason he lost was that his opponent—this giant fardel named Leona Tisdale—went knocking on people's doors at all hours of the night begging for votes."

He frowned again. "Leona was a woman with no pride."

He paused. "And one of those really huge flashlights."

I reached for the door again. Earl was right. It was hopeless.

"No, Rosie. *Stay.* I know I can help you. I'm serious," Maxie insisted.

More than anything in the world, I wanted to believe him.

I took my hand off the door. "How?"

"Trust me," said Max. "All you need to win an election is a smart campaign manager and a good platform. And I can help you with both."

I stared at him blankly. A good platform? What the heck was he talking about?

"Have you thought about it yet?" he asked. "Your campaign platform, I mean?"

I couldn't even fake an answer.

"Okay, fine. I admit it," I said. "I don't even know what a campaign platform is."

Maxie just shrugged. "No big deal. My dad explained it to me. A campaign platform is like a general statement of what you're all about. It's made up of your all viewpoints and your stands on different issues and stuff. Except, in a campaign platform, your stands on the issues are called the *planks*. Get it, Rosie? Picture the campaign platform like a big wooden floor. The floor is made up of separate floorboards, just like a campaign platform is made up of separate planks."

He thought a minute. "Let's see. Like maybe your campaign platform could be that you stand for a fair and equal chance for every student in school. And one of your planks might be—"

"Punishing all the bullies!" interrupted Earl excitedly. "I mentioned it the other day, remember? When bullies break the rules, you could throw them in a dungeon where they can't bother the rest of us. It doesn't have to be a real dungeon or anything. Just a big, dark, smelly room with no ventilation. Like the cafeteria."

Maxie gave him a dirty look. "In case you don't know it, Earl, we're being serious here."

"I do know it," said Earl. "I'm being serious, too. Okay, forget the dungeon idea. What about just a big old hole? We'll dig a big old hole in the corner of the playground. And when a kid does something mean, we'll lower him down there with a rope. And he'll have to stay in the hole for a while with a…a…

"Snake," he said.

"Earrrrrl," growled Max.

Quickly, Earl held up his hand. "No, wait. A *dingo,"* he said. "Yeah, a dingo would be better. A dingo is one of those wild dogs from Australia."

That did it. Maxie leaped over the seat and pounced right on top of him. Then the two of them fell on the floor and began wrestling all over the place. I had to get out of the car to protect myself.

Some of the time they were laughing. The rest of the time Maxie was yelling, "Ow! That hurts! Knock it off!"

Finally, Earl let him up.

Maxie's face was bright pink and he had little red blotches all over his arms. Also, his clothes were all twisted and one of his shoes had come off.

He got back in the front seat again. Then he took a deep breath and quietly muttered the same thing he always does after he gets pounded.

"I won."

Earl just smiled.

"This isn't helping, you know," I said as I climbed in the back. "Having you two wrestle the day away won't help my campaign one bit. And anyhow, why do I even need a platform, Maxie? Why can't I just hang up a bunch of posters that say ROSIE SWANSON FOR PRESIDENT, like everyone else does? No one else ever has a stupid platform."

Maxie didn't answer for a minute, but I could tell there was something on his mind.

"Well?" I asked again.

"I don't know exactly how to say this, Rosie. But just think about it a second," he said. "You're going to be running against the two most popular kids in the fourth grade. One of them is a star soccer player, and the other one looks like a model. If all you do is hang up a few posters, who do you think is going to win?"

I hid my face behind my hands and groaned.

"Stop that and listen to what I'm telling you," he said. "If you give people a good enough reason to vote for you, you don't have to be a great athlete or a beauty queen to win an election."

Earl nodded. "He's right, Rosie. I did a report on Thomas Jefferson once, and he had the biggest nostrils I've ever seen. I mean it. The man could fit an ear of corn up his nose."

"Thank you, Earl. I feel much better now," I said.

Maxie wouldn't give up. "Come on, Rosie. Earl and I can help you win this. I swear. The three of us will work on your campaign platform together. You know what they say—three heads are better than one. Right?"

I looked over at Earl.

He was measuring his nostrils.

I groaned again.

4 THANK YOU, NORMAN BEEMAN

I don't pout forever. I try my hardest. But usually I can only last for two or three days. Once, I pouted for over a week and a half, but that was pretty unusual. The red light was out at the end of my street, and my mother wouldn't let me direct traffic.

After I got home from the garage that day, I curled up in my grandfather's big easy chair and thought about what Maxie had said. All that stuff about how it was really possible for me to win and all.

I lay on my bed and closed my eyes. Before I knew it, I was imagining myself on the school stage again with that same American flag draped behind me. The crowd was going crazy, cheering and stuff. When I bowed, the gold crown I was wearing almost fell off my head.

I smiled. I realize that the president of fourth

grade doesn't actually get to wear a gold crown. But still, it's a nice fantasy.

By the time the candidates met again on Monday morning, I was feeling a little more positive about things. The meeting was called so that Mr. Jolly and Mrs. Munson could tell us more about how to run our campaigns.

It wasn't a long meeting. Mostly, they just told us about making campaign buttons and posters and junk. They said that there was no limit on the number of posters you could make, but they had to be in good taste. Good taste means no blood or cusswords.

Also, they told us that there were ninety-five kids in the fourth grade (forty-four boys and fifty-one girls), so that's how many campaign buttons we should make.

The whole time they were talking, Louise the Disease was sitting in the middle of the room with this real annoyed expression on her face. It looked like she was about to blow up or something. She practically did, too. As soon as Mr. Jolly stopped talking, Louise shot right out of her chair.

"Could someone please tell Robert Moneypenny he's not allowed to pass out real money," she said. "He says his campaign buttons are going to be pennies, but that's not allowed, is it?"

She spun around and pointed her finger in Robert's face. "You can't pass out real money, Robert. That's just like buying votes. And in this country you're not allowed to buy votes. This is America, mister."

Mr. Jolly started to grin. Meanwhile, Mrs. Munson informed Robert that he'd have to use fake pennies instead of real ones.

"See? Told ya so," said Louise the Disease.

After that, Mr. Jolly went on to explain more about the election. "In addition to making your campaign posters and buttons, there will be two meetings with the entire fourth grade," he said. "The first meeting will be held next week. It will be called 'Meet the Candidates.' You will introduce yourselves to the class and talk a little bit about your campaigns. Directly after the first meeting, you will be given time to start hanging your posters."

Mr. Jolly looked down at his notes. "The second meeting will be on Election Day. That's the day some of you will give your campaign speeches. As it gets closer to the election, Mrs. Munson and I will be available to help you with your thoughts."

Mrs. Munson looked at the clock. "Any questions?" she asked. "The bell is about to ring, so we'll have to make them quick."

Summer Lynne Jones raised her hand. "Is it okay if our friends help us make our posters? We don't have to do all the work by ourselves, do we? I was thinking about having a big poster party and inviting a bunch of kids over to help me."

Mr. Jolly nodded. "That's a great idea, Summer. The more kids that we can involve in this election, the better."

"How 'bout my soccer team?" asked Alan Allen. "It's not a school soccer team, but can I still use our picture in my poster? I've got this really awesome picture where the guys are carrying me around on their shoulders at the last game. It was in the newspaper, too. Maybe you saw it."

Mr. Jolly smiled. "I didn't see it, Alan. But go ahead and use it if you want to."

Finally, Roxanne asked the most important question of the day.

"Are you allowed to vote for yourself?" she called out.

Mrs. Munson seemed surprised. "Of course, Roxanne. I'm sure that each one of you thinks that you're the best candidate for the job, so of course you can vote for yourself."

"How many times?" I asked.

Everybody laughed.

It wasn't a joke.

For the rest of the day, the election was all I could think about. I couldn't concentrate on my school-work at all. When Judith Topper turned around to sneak a peek at my math, I didn't even have any answers for her to copy.

Maxie was right. Unless I could give everyone a good reason to vote for me, I wouldn't stand a chance. I'm not a great athlete like Alan Allen. I don't have enough friends to have a big poster party.

Still, I didn't want to quit. Quitting would have meant giving up my dream of ever being on top. And even though I knew it would be hard, I kept picturing myself with that gold crown on my head.

Think, Rosie, I told myself as I stared at my math page. *Think of a way to get some votes.* But no matter how hard I tried, I couldn't come up with anything that sounded exciting enough.

I mean, there are lots of new rules and stuff that I'd like to see happen. Like imagine how much nicer lunch would be if it was against school rules for kids to laugh until milk comes out their nose. The trouble is, hardly anyone feels as strongly about this problem as I do.

Anyway, I was just sort of mulling over some of this stuff, when I happened to glance over at Norman Beeman. He was doubled over at his desk, and his face looked greener than usual. At first, I thought he was searching for something on the floor. But then he started hugging his stomach and going "Ooooo Ooooo." So I got the picture pretty fast.

Ruthie Firestone got the picture, too. She tried to make a getaway. But she was only a step or two down the aisle when Norman's lunch came up all over the place...including a few little splats that landed on the back of Ruthie Firestone's left leg.

I won't go into all the details of what followed, except to say that Ruthie Firestone went off the deep end. She started running all around the room screaming, "GET IT OFF ME! GET IT OFF ME!" Which was so ridiculous, because no fourth-grader in their right mind is going to help you out in that situation. Finally, Ruthie Firestone ran out the door and we never saw her again.

All in all, Norman handled the situation pretty coolly, I think. Without saying a word, he went to the boys' room and cleaned up. He was back in time to watch Mr. Jim, the custodian, come in with his bucket on wheels.

"You the one who did this?" Mr. Jim asked.

Norman nodded. "What do you expect? It was Salisbury steak and peas," he said.

Anyway, the weird part about all of it was that Norman Beeman's sick stomach saved the day for me. I'm not kidding. Because of Norman, by the end of the day, I knew *exactly* what my campaign platform would be.

"I've got it! I've got it!" I hollered when I saw Maxie and Earl on the playground after school. "I've really, really got it!"

"Got what?" asked Maxie.

I looked around and lowered my voice. When you've got an idea as great as mine, you can't go blabbing it for all the world to hear.

"The perfect campaign platform, that's what," I told him. "Wait'll you hear it, you guys. Just wait'll you hear it. I'll tell you as soon as it's safe."

I made them wait until we got all the way to my house. I don't know how I held it in that long. It's a miracle I didn't swell up and explode.

When we finally got to my front porch, I started dancing all around. "Before I tell you, I'll give you a hint," I teased. "Today during math, Norman Beeman tossed his cookies."

Earl covered his mouth with his hand. Maxie just looked confused.

"Okay, okay, here's hint number two," I said. "He'd eaten a hot lunch from the cafeteria."

"I don't know," said Maxie. "I give up. What, what?"

"Cafeteria food!" I yelled excitedly. "My platform will be to improve cafeteria food, Max! Just think about it! Cafeteria food is perfect!"

Earl scrunched up his face. "Cafeteria food is perfect? Are you nuts? Last week my mother made me buy the Alpo platter. It was some kind of shiny meat with brown-looking jelly gunk on top."

He shivered a little and pulled out his pack of Rolaids.

I clapped my hands together. "Yes! But that's exactly why it's perfect, Earl," I said. "Don't you get it? Cafeteria food is gross, and I'm going to be the candidate to make it better! *That's* the reason kids will vote for me!"

I put my arm around Earl's shoulder. "I've even thought of a slogan for my campaign buttons already. Listen to this:

"ROSIE SWANSON—FOR YOUR TUMMY'S SAKE."

Maxie smiled a little. "Hmmm. That's not too bad," he said. "And maybe instead of making the buttons round, we could make them in the shape of little stomachs. Like those pink stomachs they show on Pepto-Bismol commercials. What do you think?"

What did I think? I loved it so much I lifted him right off the ground.

Maxie kept his arms at his sides like a statue.

He hates being picked up. Last year a couple of sixth-graders held him over their heads and passed him around the playground, and it's left him bitter.

After I put him down, the three of us went inside and tried to come up with poster ideas. I made Earl my official art director. Art is Earl's best subject. You should see the stuff he draws. One time he drew a picture of a monster's foot stepping on the school that looked totally real.

He started doodling a little bit, and in no time at all, he came up with the first poster idea. It was pretty neat-looking, too. It was the same monster's foot he's so good at, only this time it was about to crush a little carton of milk with steam coming off it. Across the top of the poster, he printed:

ROSIE SAYS:

STAMP OUT WARM MILK.

I started to hug him, but he pointed his finger at me. "Don't even think about it, missy," he said.

After that, we really got down to work. For

the rest of the afternoon, the three of us drove ourselves nuts trying to come up with clever ideas and poems about cafeteria food. We wanted to mention all of the food that kids hate most, but none of it seemed to rhyme that good.

Earl kept saying stuff like, "I'd rather eat a parrot than a carrot." I finally had to hit him to get him to stop.

Anyway, after about two hours, we were all starting to get headaches when suddenly Maxie sat up and blurted out,

"The French fries are fine,
The fruit cup is better.
But don't eat the peas,
Or you'll ralph on your sweater."

I grinned. "Hey. That's good, Maxie. I mean, that's really, really—"

Before I could finish, another poem popped right out of his mouth:

"Please don't make us
Eat Salisbury steakus!"

Earl and I laughed out loud.

"Quick!" said Maxie. "Write these down! I think I'm having a burst of genius here or something."

I grabbed my paper and got ready to write, but Maxie's spurt seemed to be over.

"Come on. Keep going, Max," I urged. "What about that shiny meat Earl was talking about?"

"Yeah," said Earl. "The Alpo platter. The menu called it meat loaf, but it smelled more like feet loaf."

We all cracked up over that one. I wrote it down.

The meat loaf
Smells like feet loaf!

Earl took a piece of paper and drew a smelly foot on a dinner plate. Then he covered it with gravy and drew a lump of mashed potatoes on the side.

The whole time he was drawing, I was laughing. "That looks almost as gross as those corn dogs they had on Friday. Ever wonder about those things? I mean, what the heck are they, anyway? They sort of remind me of a—"

Earl covered his mouth. "Please," he begged. "Don't."

After that, the three of us started wondering about corn dogs and what they were made of and stuff. Maxie and I began making up this funny, gross poem about them. It ended up being our best idea of the day. We called it "Dear Mr. Corn Dog":

Dear Mr. Corn Dog,
What are you...really?
Your inside is meaty,
Your outside is mealy.

Are you a yo-yo?
Was it a clue,
When I ate you at noon,
And you came up at two?

I heaved on the playground,
I'm still feeling sick.
Now all I've got left of my lunch
Is your stick.

Dear Mr. Corn Dog,
I'm not being nosy,
But what are you...really?
Sincerely yours,
Rosie

5 STAR-SPANGLED ME

It was the day before the "Meet the Candidates" meeting, and I was really getting excited. Earl and Maxie and I had spent hours making posters, and I couldn't wait to hang them in the halls so everyone could see them. No one loves disgusting poems and posters more than fourth-graders.

In fact, everything was going so well I was feeling spunky, almost. And, I'm sorry, but sometimes when you're feeling spunky, you can't help bragging a teeny bit. Especially when you're standing behind Alan Allen in the drinking fountain line…and he looks directly right at you…and he doesn't even say hello. An insult like that can even make you mad, if you want to know the truth.

Alan Allen is arrogant. It's a word I learned from Maxie. It means you're so self-confident, you're annoying. Arrogant people go around with this certain look on their faces. It's almost a grin, but not quite. It's the kind of look that makes people want to smack you.

I didn't smack him, though. Instead, I tapped him on the shoulder so he couldn't ignore me anymore.

"So, how's the old campaign going, Al?" I asked. "Been working on your posters much?"

At first, Alan stared at me like he was trying to figure out who I was. Then he shrugged and said, "Nah."

"Oh really?" I said. "Well, if I were you, I'd get busy, Al. 'Cause my friends and I have been working on *my* posters a lot."

Alan didn't reply.

"A *real* lot, I mean," I added. "In fact, I've got two fifth-graders working on my campaign around the clock. Maybe you've heard of them. Earl Wilber and Maxie Zuckerman? Earl is like the best artist in the entire fifth grade. And Maxie's practically an Einstein or something. So you can imagine the great poster ideas we've come up with."

"Gee," said Alan. "I'm *so* worried."

"Yeah, well, too bad I can't tell you what the posters are about, Al. But my ideas are so great I'm keeping them a secret until the 'Meet the Candidates' meeting tomorrow."

Alan took a drink and looked back at me. "Don't call me Al," he said.

"Okay, fine. All I'm telling you is that I've got a great campaign going," I said. "And that's not bragging, either, Al. 'Cause my grandfather says something's only bragging if it's not true. And what I'm saying is all true. I've got an unbelievable campaign going. Seriously. I do."

Alan wiped his mouth. "I'm shakin'," he said. Then he turned and ran back out to the soccer field.

I smiled a little and leaned down to get some water. He could act as cool as he wanted to, but I could tell that I'd gotten to him.

As I was drinking, someone tapped me on my shoulder. "What were you two talking about just now?"

When I stood up, Summer Lynne Jones was standing behind me. She'd probably been listening the whole time.

Casual as anything, I shrugged. "Oh, nothing," I said. "It's just that my campaign for president is going really great. And Alan's getting a little worried, I guess."

I leaned a little closer to her. "I mean, it's going *really* great, Summer," I added. "*Amazingly* great."

I almost grinned, but not quite. "Well…ta ta, Summer. See you on-stage tomorrow," I said.

After that, I strolled away without even looking back.

That afternoon my grandfather picked me up from school. My mother said I could buy a special outfit to wear to the candidates' meeting, so Granddad offered to take me to the mall.

When it comes to shopping, my grandfather and I get along a lot better than my mom and I do. That's because my mother is always trying to buy me things a kindergarten kid would wear. Also, if I find two outfits that I really love, she hardly ever lets me get both of them. Not even if I cry and promise not to ask for another thing for the rest of my life.

Granddad is way easier to deal with. He sits in a chair, holds my jacket, and goes to sleep. Once, a security guard thought he was dead and poked him with a plastic hanger.

Not this time, though. This time I was so speedy my grandfather didn't even have a chance to get comfortable. The outfit I wanted was right on the mannequin in the girls' department. It was a red, white, and blue sweater with a matching navy-blue skirt. The perfect colors for an election.

It looked great on me, too. When I came out of the dressing room, the saleslady whistled and said I looked like "a million bucks."

"I'm running for president of my fourth-grade class," I told her.

She grinned. "Well, in that outfit you can't lose, sweetie. Right, Gramps?"

Granddad frowned.

"He doesn't like to be called Gramps," I whispered to the woman.

The lady frowned back at him and said, "Cash or charge?"

Anyhow, as it turned out, my mother loved the outfit I picked as much as I did. The next morning she even fixed my hair in a French braid and tied it with red, white, and blue satin ribbons.

When I got to Maxie's house, Earl said I looked like the Star-Spangled Banner. He didn't laugh when he said it, so I knew it was a compliment.

As we were walking to school, he dug into his jeans and held his hand out to me. "Here. I found these this morning. They were growing through a crack in my driveway."

He opened his fist. In his hand were two lucky four-leaf clovers.

I started to take both of them, but Earl shook his head. "No, no, no. You only get *one*," he said. "I need the other one to get through my own little problem today."

It made me smile. Earl almost always has some kind of little problem going on.

"Well, I guess this is it, huh, guys? Today's the big day, right? I hope my speech goes okay. I mean, I hope I don't get all tongue-tied and say something stupid."

I paused and waited for them to tell me I wouldn't. But as usual, they didn't.

Instead, Maxie held the posters and the bag of campaign buttons closer to his body. Even though the posters were wrapped in black plastic, he was worried that someone would see them.

"Quit worrying, Maxie," I said. "It's too late for anyone to steal our posters or copy our campaign ideas now. My ideas are going to knock their socks off. That's what my mother calls it when you really surprise people. She calls it knocking their socks off."

Maxie looked all around. "I hope so," he said, sounding unsure.

I gave him a shove. "We will, we will. And don't worry about me dumping you guys after I win, either. Once I'm president, I'm going to make you my fifth-grade advisers."

Maxie forced a smile. He never stopped looking around, though. He was guarding those posters with his life.

When we finally got to school, the bell was already ringing. Maxie was so relieved to hand me the posters and campaign buttons he practically shoved them at me.

Meanwhile, Earl started acting even weirder

than Max. Instead of taking off for his classroom, he stood in front of me, rocking back and forth on his feet. It was like there was something he wanted to tell me, but he just couldn't get it out.

Finally, he just blurted, "Good luck," and he rushed through the door.

When I looked around, Maxie was gone, too.

The candidates' meeting was at nine-thirty. Mr. Jolly dismissed me at nine o'clock so I could "go freshen up and get ready." In a way, it was sort of insulting. I mean, couldn't he see that I was already *ready?* My hair was beautiful and I was dressed like the Star-Spangled Banner. How much better could I possibly look?

I didn't make a big deal about it, though. I just went into the girls' bathroom and sat on the sink for a while. Then, finally, I wandered over to the media center.

Nic and Vic Timmerman were already there. Their hair was all slicked down with gel and they had on matching bow ties. They were searching for their name tags on their seats at the long candidates' table in the front of the room.

I thought about talking to them. But then Louise the Disease came in, so I talked to her instead. I know this sounds mean, but I'd rather catch a cold than be seen with two bizarros like Nic and Vic.

One by one, the audience started to arrive. As they did, the other candidates came in and found their seats at the big table. When everyone was finally seated, all the candidates for class secretary were at one end, and all the presidents were at the other end. The treasurers and vice presidents were in the middle.

Summer Lynne Jones sat in the chair on my right at the very end of the table. Even though it was sort of chilly outside, she was wearing sandals, a straw hat, and a bright yellow sundress. I think she wanted to look "summery."

"You look like a flag," she said when she sat down.

"Thank you," I answered. But this time I was sure it wasn't a compliment. Competitors never compliment each other on the way they look. Like you never hear a boxer get into the ring and say, "Yo, Rocky...love your shorts."

Alan Allen was the last candidate to arrive. He strolled in the room acting totally cool and sat down on my left. He waved to a couple of his friends and snickered, sort of. But when I turned to look at him, he looked away.

All of a sudden, Mrs. Munson clapped her hands together to begin the meeting.

"May I have your attention, please?" she asked. "As your teachers have explained, this morning we are going to have an opportunity to meet the candidates running for class office. During the past few days, we have been talking to you about the political process and how it works. As we have told you, the job you have as voters is the most important job there is. You have the awesome responsibility of choosing the best person for each office. So it's up to you to find out as much about the candidates and their views as you can.

"This morning the candidates are going to introduce themselves to you and tell you a little bit about themselves and their campaigns. We will begin with Roxanne Handleman, who is running for class secretary."

Roxanne gasped. "No," she said. "No way!"

Mrs. Munson frowned. "Excuse me, Roxanne?" she asked. "Is there something the matter?"

"Why me? Why do I have to go first?" asked Roxanne. "How come we can't just raise our hands when we're ready to talk? I thought we were gonna get to raise our hands."

Mr. Jolly walked over to Roxanne and leaned down. "There's nothing to be nervous about," he said quietly. "We just want to know a little bit about you and why you're running. We talked about this before, remember?"

"Yeah, I know. But nobody said I had to go first. I thought we were gonna get to raise our hands. The first one always flubs up."

Mr. Jolly narrowed his eyes. "Roxanne. Please. Just go."

Roxanne stood up. "Okay, okay. I'll go. But I still don't think this is fair."

She took a deep breath. "My name is Roxanne Handleman and I'm running for class secretary because, well...I don't exactly know why. I just wanted to, that's all. I mean, no one told me I had to have a reason. But lots of people do stuff without knowing why. That doesn't mean they're not good at it, though. Like my brother can't stand to have his vegetables touching his meat. But that doesn't mean he's not a good eater. And so I'd be a good secretary, too, probably. It's just that I didn't know I needed a reason.

"The end," she said.

She sat down, put her head on the table, and covered up with her arms.

Next to her, Karla something jumped right up. She didn't even wait to be called on.

"My name is Karla Ungerman and I'm running for class secretary because my mother—Mrs. Sharla Ungerman—is a secretary at the high school and she's teaching me how to type. Also, I'm very organized. Plus, ever since first grade I've gotten straight A's in English and penmanship."

Karla sat down for a second, then popped right back up again. "Oops! I almost forgot—I also get straight A's in spelling."

This time when she sat, she smoothed her dress neatly and lowered herself gracefully into her chair.

Roxanne raised her head. "Big whoop," she snapped.

The candidates for treasurer came next. Louise the Disease held up her new calculator for everyone to see. "I just got this for my birthday and I already know how to use it," she said.

After that, she turned to Robert Moneypenny and smirked. "Even the *memory feature,* Robert," she said.

Robert leaned his chair back on two legs and raised his fists in the air. "ROBERT MONEY-PENNY FOR TREASURER!" he shouted out.

After that, all the boys started waving their fists, too, and making that stupid gorilla noise. The one that sounds like "hoo hoo hoo hoo hoo hoo."

During the commotion, Vic Timmerman stood up and blurted, "I'm Victor Timmerman and I'm a whiz with numbers." But I'm pretty sure no one heard him.

I don't remember what any of the candidates for vice president said. By that time, I was too nervous to pay much attention. All I know for sure is that when we got to the presidents, Summer Lynne Jones said a few words about how she'd be our friend in government, and then she tossed her long blond hair around for a while.

When it finally got to Alan Allen, the room practically went wild. I mean it. His friends started chanting his name and they wouldn't stop.

"Allllan…Allllan…Allllan…Allllan…Allllan…"

After a while, Alan raised his hands to quiet the crowd. A second later, he pulled a piece of paper from his shirt pocket and began to read:

> "'A Campaign Poem,'
> by Alan Allen.
>
> The French fries are fine,
> The fruit cup is better.
> But don't eat the peas,
> Or you'll ralph on your sweater."

He looked up from his paper and started clapping for himself. "Alan Allen for better lunches!" he shouted.

I fell off my chair.

6 HARD FEELINGS

I caught myself before I hit the floor.

"Hey! Wait a minute! Hold it! That was *my* poem! He stole it, Mr. Jolly! He stole my poem!"

I stood up and stamped my foot. Mrs. Munson rushed up to the candidates' table and ordered me to sit down again. I guess I must have done it, but I really don't remember much. I was boiling over inside. Madder than I've ever been in my whole life, I mean.

The meeting came to a quick close. Mrs. Munson and Mr. Jolly met with Alan and me. Just the four of us.

"Tell us about the poem, Alan," Mr. Jolly said.

As usual, Alan tried to act real cool and all. But he finally admitted that the poem was mine.

"I didn't really steal it, though," he said. "I just

borrowed it, sort of. Just to recite at the meeting today."

"Borrowed it?" I yelled. "You don't borrow a poem, Alan. I didn't even give you permission. You stole it!"

"I did not! I didn't steal anything," he insisted. "One of your friends spouted it out all over the place. If you don't believe me, just ask him. It's that geeky fifth-grader you hang out with. And anyway, my father told me that in political campaigns, people use each other's ideas all the time. So I thought it would be okay."

Mr. Jolly rolled his eyes. "Stealing a poem wasn't what your father meant, Alan. I think you know that. The poem was Rosie's. You owe her a big apology."

I stamped my foot again. "No, Mr. Jolly! No! I don't want an apology. I want Alan to drop out of the race. I worked hard on my campaign about cafeteria food, and now everyone will think that I'm copying him! He shouldn't be able to run. He just shouldn't."

Mr. Jolly stared at Alan some more. Mrs. Munson just sat there tapping her foot. I mean, please! What was there to think about? Why didn't they just kick him out?

Mr. Jolly ran his fingers through his hair. "I don't know, Rosie," he said. "We all agree that it was wrong that Alan recited your poem. But I'm not sure we should make him quit the race."

He looked at Mrs. Munson. "I'm not even sure we can forbid him to campaign for better cafeteria food."

A knot formed in my stomach. "Yes! You can! You're *teachers*. You can forbid anything you want to."

Mrs. Munson sighed. "The thing is, Rosie, Alan's father may be right about this. This is politics. And in politics, if one candidate comes up with a good idea, you can't forbid the other candidates from using it, too."

"You need to understand this, Rosie," Mr. Jolly said. "Let's say that two men are running for president of the United States, and one of them decides he'll lower taxes. Well, if the other candidate thinks that lowering taxes will be a popular idea with the voters, then he might begin to campaign for it, too. In our system, he's allowed to do that."

I turned my eyes away from him.

Mrs. Munson took over from there. "Mr. Jolly is correct, Rosie," she said. "And while we certainly won't let Alan use your poems or copy your poster ideas, he is allowed to campaign for better lunches. If Alan thinks it's a good idea, then he's allowed to jump on the bandwagon, so to speak."

Alan was practically puffing out with glee. You should have seen him. You could have popped him with a pin.

"I'm sorry I recited your poem," he said. "But I still like the idea about making the cafeteria food better. No hard feelings, okay?" he said.

"Oh yes, there are, Alan," I replied. "There're *lots* of hard feelings. More hard feelings than you can even count."

After that, I narrowed my eyes at Mrs. Munson and Mr. Jolly. And I walked out of the room.

I saw Earl on the playground at recess. He was crouching behind a tree trying to hide from me. It was all the confession I needed.

I took off running in his direction.

"You can't hide from me, Earl! I know it was you! I'm coming to kill you, Earl."

Maxie was standing next to him. When he saw me coming, he backed up a little bit.

By the time I got to the tree, Earl had put his sweater over his head. I yanked it off him and crouched down next to his face.

"IT WAS SUPPOSED TO BE A SECRET, EARL! IT WAS SUPPOSED TO BE A SECRET!"

Furiously, I took his four-leaf clover out of my pocket and threw it at his face.

"No wonder you wanted me to have this! No wonder you needed one for yourself! You and your 'little problem.' You were hoping I wouldn't find out, but I did!"

"Stupid clovers," muttered Earl quietly. "I knew that good-luck junk was a bunch of hogwash."

Finally, he looked up at me. "I'm sorry, Rosie. I'm really, really sorry. But they made me tell them. They did. I swear."

I had to bite my lip to keep from crying. That's how mad I was. And disappointed, too.

"Who, Earl?" I managed. "Who made you tell? Who made you ruin my whole entire campaign?"

His answer took me by surprise.

"Summer Lynne Jones," he said. "Summer Lynne Jones and that friend of hers with the long black hair. They ran up behind me while I was walking home from school yesterday and started asking a bunch of stuff about your campaign."

"Like what *kind* of stuff?" I asked.

He shrugged. "All kinds of stuff," he said. "Like why you kept bragging that your campaign was so good. And what kind of posters I was drawing."

"And so you just *told* her, Earl? You just spilled your guts about our campaign? Just because she *asked?*"

"No," he said. "At first, I didn't tell her anything at all. At first, I said we were keeping it a secret until the candidates' meeting."

I folded my arms. "So then how did she find out?"

Earl swallowed hard. "Well, we were just standing around in the grass. And then the one

71

with the long black hair patted the ground. You know, for me to sit down."

"So?"

"So I sat."

"And?"

Earl lowered his voice again. "And then Summer asked me if I was ticklish. And even though I said no, she and her friend started tickling me anyway. And you know how much I hate that, Rosie. But they kept tickling and tickling. And they said they wouldn't stop until I told them about your posters."

I couldn't stand to listen to this. "Oh, Earl."

"I know, I know. But I couldn't help it, Rosie. Tickling is torture, almost. Plus, rolling in the grass was making me wheezy. And my nose was getting all plugged up and I couldn't breathe. I *had* to tell them, Rosie. I was suffocating, practically."

Now I was angry all over again.

"No, you weren't, Earl. You weren't suffocating. And being tickled is no excuse. What kind of traitor spills his guts to the enemy and then runs back to the general and says, 'Sorry, General. I was tickled'?"

I pushed him. "Do you know what happened because of you, Earl? Summer Jones told Alan Allen all about my campaign. And Alan Allen stood right up in front of the entire fourth grade this morning and recited one of my poems. And now he's going to campaign for better lunches. And Mr. Jolly is letting him!"

Tears started to fill my eyes. "Darn it, Earl! Why did you have to tell?"

Earl sat there for a second, just sort of staring off into space. Then all of a sudden, he got a funny look on his face.

"No. Wait a second. That can't be right. How could he have recited one of our poems? I didn't tell Summer Lynne any of our poems."

"Yes, you did! You did, too, Earl! You told her the one about the fruit cup and the French fries, because that's the poem he recited. If you didn't tell her, then how else would Alan have known it?"

Not saying a word, Maxie quietly turned and started walking toward the school.

It took a second before it finally hit me.

I ran after him and spun him around.

As soon as I looked at his face, I knew.

"It was *you*," I said in amazement. "You're the one who told Alan my poem."

Maxie's face changed.

"So what? So what if it was me? I don't care what you say. I'm sick of getting insulted by kids like Alan Allen. Sixth-graders are bad enough. But Alan's only a *fourth*-grader and he was pushing me around."

Maxie's eyes narrowed. "He and his friends called me Poindexter! And a dweeb. And he said if I was such a brainiac, then how come I couldn't figure out how to grow?"

Maxie pointed to Earl. "And he made fun of Earl, too. He said Earl couldn't draw worth spit. 'Earl Wilber is a doofus,' he says. 'My posters are going to kill your posters. Kill 'em, Zuckerman,' he says.

"So I just try to be cool about it, you know? And I say, 'Oh yeah? We'll just see about that, Alan.' And I start to walk away.

"Except then, a couple of his friends grab me and start spinning me in a circle until I can't walk straight. And then Alan puts his arm around my shoulders like suddenly we're pals. And he walks me over to the corner of the parking lot.

"'Okay,' he says. 'I'll make you a deal, Maxie. I'll tell you a secret about me, and then you can tell me your campaign secret. That way we'll be even.'

"Then he whispers this stupid secret about how he stole a soccer ball from Mort's Sports Store when he was in the first grade.

"So I say, 'Big deal, Alan. What good's a stupid secret like that going to do us? I'm not telling you anything.' And that's when Alan really gets mad. And he grabs the front of my shirt with both of his fists and starts slinging me around a little bit. And he's getting me totally wrinkled. And so I say, 'Knock it off, Alan. My mother just ironed this shirt!'

"And he looks at me like I was a lunatic or something. And he says, 'God! How can such a skinny wimp be such a giant dork! Huh! I mean, how is that even scientifically possible?'

"And then he hits himself in the head and says, 'What the heck was I so worried about? There's no way in the world that you and that fat tub of goo, Earl Wilber, will be able to get your geeky girlfriend elected president of the fourth grade. No way.'

"After that, he let go of me and shoved me

backward. And I was so mad I could spit. And so I took a giant step right into his face. And then I stood on my toes until our noses were almost touching and I said, 'Oh yeah? Well, laugh about this, you snool. 'Cause this is what's going to blow your campaign right out of the water!' And then I blurted out the fruit cup poem."

Maxie stopped and took a breath. "Look, I *know* I shouldn't have done it, okay? And I wish it never happened. But I was so sick and tired of being picked on that day, I just had to make them stop."

The bell rang. Maxie and Earl didn't go in. Neither did I.

Instead, I sat down in the grass and pulled my knees up to hide my face.

Earl came over and tapped me on the shoulder. "Come on, Rosie. We've gotta go."

I knocked his hand away.

"So go," I said.

And they did.

7 THE AMERICAN WAY

I didn't speak to Maxie or Earl for two days. I wanted to hold out longer, but not walking to school with them was driving me crazy. If I don't walk with them, they never use the crosswalks.

Friday morning, I finally showed up at Maxie's house. It was kind of awkward at first. Mostly, we just stood around and looked at each other. We haven't really been friends that long, so we're still learning how to do it.

Finally, Maxie waved stiffly and said hi.

"Hi," I said back.

"Hi," said Earl.

After that, all of us stood there some more. Then, without any warning at all, Earl bent over and butted me with his head. I don't know why he does stuff like that. It's just the way his mind works. It did the trick, though. It made us laugh and loosen up a little.

We didn't have a big discussion about how they'd let me down or anything. Mostly, I just told them to forget about it. It was big of me to act like that, I thought. I told them that, too. "This is big of me," I said.

What I didn't tell them is that way deep down inside, I knew that part of what had happened was my fault, too. I mean, if I hadn't been so braggy at the drinking fountain that day, Alan and Summer wouldn't have been so curious about my campaign.

Anyhow, I was glad to finally have my friends back again. At school, things had been getting harder and harder to deal with. Like Alan's posters were going up all over the place. And just as I thought, they were about cafeteria food.

They weren't as good as mine, though. Most of his posters were just boring old pictures of pizza cut out of magazines. His slogan was stupid, too:

WANT PIZZA AND COKE?
GIVE ALAN YOUR VOTE!

I mean, come on. Coke and vote don't even rhyme. And here's another dumb thing. Alan's campaign buttons were little pepperonis. If you pinned them to your shirt, they left an oil stain.

Even Norman Beeman liked my stuff better. He plodded right up to me in the hall and said, "Your posters are way neater than his."

I looked down at his feet. "Thank you, Norman," I said. "Love your boots."

Even Summer Lynne Jones's campaign buttons were better than Alan's. And at least Summer hadn't stolen my ideas. Actually, she told Earl that she thought my food poems were revolting.

Instead, her posters were pictures of people at the beach doing "summery" things. At the top of every poster, there was a picture of the sun wearing sunglasses. It said:

KIDS LOVE SUMMER THE BEST!

Like a lot of girls I know, Summer dots her *i*'s with little hearts. Talk about revolting.

Her campaign buttons were little paper-doll swimsuits made of different-colored construction paper. They even had tabs on them like real paper-doll clothes.

The girls loved them, too. When Summer passed them out after the candidates' meeting, I could actually hear girls squealing because they were so cute.

Still, out of all the candidates, Louise the Disease's campaign was the absolute stupidest. All her posters said the very same thing:

LOUISE MARIE SMYTHE—

SHE COMES WITH HER OWN CALCULATOR.

It made her sound like a doll you'd get for Christmas. I'm surprised she didn't add, "Batteries not included."

She didn't stand a chance against Robert Moneypenny. His posters were cooler than anything. Each one had a snapshot of Robert leaning back in an easy chair, with his feet propped up on a big desk. And underneath each picture it said:

MONEYPENNY FOR TREASURER

THE NAME SAYS IT ALL. . .

Except for Alan Allen, Karla something turned out to be the meanest person running for office.

Her posters were sort of vicious, if you want to know the truth. They said stuff like:

ROXANNE HANDLEMAN GOT A "D" IN PENMANSHIP.

And:

ASK ROXANNE HANDLEMAN ABOUT HER GRADE IN SPELLING.

They didn't stay up long, though. As soon as Mr. Jolly saw them, he called a short candidates' meeting and told us that dirty campaigning and "mudslinging" were not allowed. He said that even though it happens in real campaigns, elementary schools should have higher standards than our nation's leaders.

Anyway, I never thought I'd say this, but making posters turned out to be one of the easiest parts of running for office. The hardest part was how I had to go around being nice to people all the time. And how I had to always keep smiling.

I'm not kidding. I even had to smile at kids who make me sick.

Maxie said it's called "sucking up." He said it's the American way.

Sometimes I smiled till my cheeks ached. Once I had to go into the girls' room and massage my face muscles. But even after all that, it didn't seem like it was making much of a difference.

"I don't think this cheery stuff is working," I said to Maxie one afternoon. "Hardly anybody ever smiles back. And besides, when you go around grinning all the time, kids think you're a sicko or something. Yesterday I was standing around smiling at a bunch of kids in the lunch line, and this boy I didn't even know told me I was giving him the creeps."

Maxie wasn't very sympathetic. "I don't care. It doesn't matter. You have to keep smiling. Smiling is one of the main rules of politics: one, smile; two, have a firm handshake; and three, never wear a bad toupee."

Judith Topper was the hardest person for me to smile at. Just in case you forgot, Judith is the jerky, creepy girl who sits right in front of me.

Every day she came to school wearing one of Alan's stupid pepperonis. I'm positive she only did it to annoy me. Sometimes she'd even point at it and say, "Alan says we're gonna have pizza every single Friday. That's why I'm voting for *him* and not *you*."

I tried not to let her see how much it bothered me. Mostly, I'd just keep my voice calm and say, "I know, Judith. But Alan would never even have thought of the pizza idea if it wasn't for me."

"Would've, too," she'd say back.

After she turned around, I would make a gross face at the back of her head. The one where I pull down the bottoms of my eyes and stretch my mouth out with my thumbs.

I never let her see me, though. 'Cause here's the worst part of all. Even though I can't stand Judith Topper's guts, I still wanted her to vote for me.

I'm not proud about it, but it's true. That's what happens in politics. Even if a disgusting green slimeball oozed under the classroom door, you'd still want it to vote for you.

Stuff like that can make you very mixed-up inside. And sometimes when you're very mixed-up inside, you do things you know you shouldn't do.

Like I've never told anybody this. Not even Maxie. But I wanted Judith Topper's vote so bad I let her look at the answers on my state capitals test. I mean it. I actually let Judith cheat off me on purpose.

I still think about it a lot. About how I pretended to drop my pencil on the floor that day. And how I leaned down to pick it up as slowly as I could. To give her time, you know? Time to see almost any answer she wanted.

I even wrote I NEED YOUR VOTE in the margin of my paper, so she would understand that we were sort of helping each other out here.

I'm still not exactly sure what happened. Maybe it's just hard to read state capitals when they're upside down. But Judith still didn't pass the test. She put down that the capital of Delaware was Rover, instead of Dover. Like Delaware would actually name its capital after a dog. Also, she wrote that the capital of Idaho was Potato.

But what made me the sickest was that the

very next morning, she *still* came to school wearing one of Alan's pepperonis.

I put one of my little pink stomach buttons on her desk so she could switch. But instead of pinning it on, she picked it up by the very edge—like it was dirty or something—and she dropped it on the floor.

"No offense," she said, wrinkling up her nose. "But these little stomachs are the most disgusting campaign buttons I've ever seen."

This time I didn't even think about being nice. "Yeah, right, Judith. Like wearing a hunk of oily meat on your shirt is in good taste."

Judith smiled meanly. Then she started singing, "You're gonna lose." Only she sang it real loud and slow, like, "YOU'RE GONNA LUUUU-OOOOZE...YOU'RE GONNA LUUUU-OOOOZE."

Two rows over, Billie Ray Carver grabbed a pencil and hopped up on his chair. He pretended to be her conductor. You know, the orchestra guy with the stick.

I hate Billie Ray Carver. Not quite as much as Judith Topper, but still a very, very lot.

Sometimes when he walks past my desk, I hold my breath. He doesn't smell bad or anything. I just don't like to breathe in the air he's stirred up. It's filled with BRC's—Billie Ray's cooties. And I don't want them getting into my nostrils.

Anyway, the stupid thing was that the whole time Billie Ray Carver was pretending to be a conductor, he was wearing one of my campaign buttons. Not on his collar, though. He was wearing it on his stomach just to be gross.

Billie Ray really loved my buttons. Maxie said he was the best advertisement we had. "Face it, Rosie. Jerks like that have a lot of friends," he said. "You've got to suck up to Billie Ray Carver, even if it kills you."

And so that afternoon, when we went out to the playground for recess and I saw Billie Ray Carver put gum on one of the swings, I didn't say a word.

He knew I saw him, too. "Hey, Swanson," he hollered. "Want to see something funny?"

Then he called to this cute girl in our class named Anna Havana. "Hey, Anna. Come over here! I'll push you!"

And so Anna Havana went over and sat down right on the swing with the gum. And I didn't even try to warn her. I just kept my mouth shut. And I watched.

I told myself it was no big deal, you know? 'Cause Billie Ray was so important to my campaign and all. Plus, Anna's mother could get the gum off her dress pretty easy, probably. Which doesn't mean that I felt good about it or anything. I'm just telling you what I was thinking.

After recess, Billie Ray Carver stopped by my desk. "Did you see that, Swanson?" he asked. "Man, girls are such *suckers*."

I tried not to breathe in his air. "Yeah, well, if girls are such suckers, then how come you're voting for one?" I asked.

For a second, he looked really confused. Then he looked down at my campaign button on his stomach and started to laugh.

"What? Are you crazy? Just because you have the grossest campaign buttons doesn't mean I'd ever *vote* for you. News flash, Swanson. You're a four-eyed, geeky girl. No boy in his right mind would vote for you. And anyway, in case you haven't heard, Alan Allen is going to get us pizza and Coke on Fridays."

Then Billie Ray Carver leaned so close to me that billions of his cooties poured into my nostrils.

"Alllan...Alllan...Alllan...Alllan...Alllan," he said over and over.

Judith Topper spun around in her chair and joined in.

"Alllan...Alllan...Alllan...Alllan," they said together. And they just kept it up and kept it up until I didn't think I could stand it one more second.

Where was Mr. Jolly? Why wasn't he in the room yet?

"Alllan...Alllan...Alllan..."

They wanted me to cry. I know they did. I didn't do it, though. The inside of my throat ached from trying to hold back the tears, but I still didn't cry.

And then all of a sudden, this really weird thing happened. One of my hands snuck into my desk and started feeling all around in there. And then—way in the back, under my geography workbook—it finally found what it was looking for.

My fingers touched my yellow notepad.

The one I write secret notes on when it's necessary to tattle to the teacher.

I smiled a little.

I was getting an idea.

* 8 * MOON MEN

It didn't take long before I had come up with a plan. It was all so simple, I wondered why I hadn't thought of it before.

The voters had a job to do, but they just weren't doing it. Mrs. Munson had told them to find out as much as they could about the candidates so they could choose the best person for the office. But instead of caring about our backgrounds, kids like Billie Ray Carver were going to vote for Alan Allen just because he was a boy. And—even worse—kids like Judith Topper were voting for him because of a pizza idea that he practically stole from me.

Alan was a thief. And I was honest. How much clearer could it be? *I* was the better choice for president, not *him*. And if the voters weren't going to find out the truth about Alan for themselves, I would just have to help them out a little.

As soon as the coast was clear, I pulled out my notepad and wrote four short notes. They were all exactly the same:

> Dear Fourth Grade Friend,
> Alan Allen stole Rosie Swanson's campaign ideas. Also, he stole a soccer ball from Mort's Sports. Is this really the kind of person you want to elect for president of the fourth grade?
> Sincerely yours,
> The Committee Who Wants You to Be a Good Voter

I folded each one separately and stuffed it deep into my skirt pocket. Knowing what I was about to do made me scared and excited at the same time. After school, I would secretly deliver one note to each fourth-grade classroom. After that, the gossip would spread like wildfire. And—

as long as I was careful—no one would ever know that it was me who started it all.

Suddenly, a brilliant idea popped into my head. *Disguise the notes, Rosie.*

Yes! I thought. *Of course!* If I disguised the notes, no one would be able to tell they were from me.

I pulled them out of my pocket and hid them on my lap. Then carefully, I opened each one up and I dotted all the *i*'s with the little hearts. I *told* you it was brilliant. I'm the only girl I know who would never, ever do that.

I was just stuffing the last note back into my pocket when the dismissal bell rang. I didn't leave, though. Instead, I stayed in my seat and waited for everyone to clear out of the room.

It took forever, too. This kid named William Washington kept following Mr. Jolly around the room, telling him some stupid story about how his grandmother has a potato chip that looks like Abraham Lincoln.

It took almost ten minutes before William wrapped up his potato chip story. The whole time he was blabbing, I pretended to be cleaning out my desk. Finally, Mr. Jolly walked William into the hall.

That's when I made my move.

In a flash, I pulled one of the notes out of my pocket and put it on Neil McNulty's chair. Neil McNulty has the biggest mouth in the entire fourth grade. He's definitely the "go to" guy if you want to spread a rumor.

After that, I grabbed my jacket and hurried out of the room. Then—on my way down the hall—I quietly ducked into each of the other fourth-grade classrooms and stuck a note on the seat of the closest chair.

This might sound risky, but it wasn't at all. Two of the teachers weren't even there, and the other one was standing at the sink in the back of the room. It looked like she was trying to get glue out of her hair or something. She never even turned around.

Once I finally got outside the building, I started to run. I didn't stop, either. Not until I was all the way home. When I hit the front door, I ran straight up to my room and locked myself inside.

I huffed and puffed and tried to catch my breath. "The voters will thank you for this,

Rosie," I whispered to myself. "Really. They will. You'll see."

Downstairs, I could hear my mother rattling around in the kitchen. She usually gets home from work about half an hour before I do.

After a few minutes, I unlocked my door and went down. If I don't say hello to my mother when I come home from school, she comes stalking me.

Trying to act relaxed, I strolled into the kitchen and grabbed an apple out of the fruit bowl on the table.

Mom was making tuna salad for dinner. She smiled at me, and the two of us began our usual after-school conversation.

"Hi, honey. How's everything goin'?"

"Good."

"How was school today?"

"Good."

"How'd the history quiz go this morning?"

"Good."

"How's the campaign going?"

"Good."

"Good," she said. Then she went back to her salad.

I drummed my fingers on the tabletop for a minute. I smiled like there was nothing wrong. But the truth was, my stomach had started to feel tense and achy inside. I guess my nerves were finally starting to catch up with me or something. That happens sometimes. You're real brave at first, and then your nerves catch up with you.

"Mom? I've got a question about something," I said finally. "I mean, it's no big deal, really. I just want your opinion, okay?"

"About what?" she asked.

I squirmed a little. How could I word it so she wouldn't suspect anything?

"Um, well, let's just say it's sort of about..."

I paused to think a second. "...um...

"...moon men."

My mother raised her eyebrows. "Moon men?"

"Yeah, yeah. It's about moon men. I mean, let's just say there's this moon man who wants to be elected king of the moon. And he's really, really popular with the moon people. But there's something about him they don't know about. Something he did a long time ago, that was sort of...bad."

My mother folded her arms. "Like what?"

I stalled for a minute. "I don't know. Like what if he stole something from a store, but none of the voters know about it. Somebody ought to tell them, don't you think? I mean, the voters need to know about his past so they don't elect a thief, right?"

Mom looked funny at me. I'm sure she knew we weren't talking about moon men.

"How long ago did he steal it?" she asked. "And how old was he when it happened?"

I shrugged my shoulders. Where was she getting all these annoying questions?

"I don't know, Mother," I said. "What difference does it make?"

"It could make a *lot* of difference, Rosie," she said. "Maybe this guy is not really a thief at all. Maybe he just made a mistake, and it was a long time ago, and he learned his lesson. In fact, maybe it made him feel so bad, he's just as honest—or even *more* honest—than anyone else on the moon."

I threw my head back. "No, Mother. No, no, no. That's just stupid. How can somebody who's stolen something be more honest than someone who's never, ever stolen anything in her whole entire life?"

My mom stared at me curiously. Then she took one of those long, deep breaths that mothers always take when they're trying to brace themselves for bad news.

"Okay, kiddo," she said. "Let's have it. What's this all about?"

I stood up. "Nothing. It's not about anything. It was just a stupid question about a stupid moon man, and I don't want to talk about it any-stupid-more."

Then, before she could ask anything else, I hurried out the door and headed toward the stairs. Halfway there, I looked back over my shoulder. I couldn't believe she wasn't following me. Usually when I act like that, she's right on my heels.

As soon as I got to my room, I locked my door again. Sometimes adults don't make any sense at all. I mean, who the heck cares how old Alan was when he stole the soccer ball? Even a baby thief is still a thief, isn't he? And besides, it was pretty clear that Alan hadn't learned his lesson about stealing. He'd stolen my poem right out of Maxie's mouth.

Just then, there was a knock on my door. I knew it! I knew she'd follow me!

"Rosie? Can I come in? What's wrong? Did one of the other candidates steal something? Was it Alan?"

I forced my voice to sound normal. "No. It's nothing. Just never mind, okay? I'm taking a nap."

There was a pause.

"Rosie."

"I'm asleep."

I listened closely. Mom sat down on the floor and leaned her back up against my door. "Suit yourself, but I'm not going away until you tell me what's going on," she said.

I made a loud snoring sound.

"Come on, Rosie. I mean it. Let me in. I want to help."

I covered my head with my blanket. "You can't help, Mother," I said. "Nobody can. You don't have a magic wand, do you? Do you have a magic wand that will make me pretty and popular?"

I knew what she would say. It's the same thing

every mother in the world says at times like this. It must be in the official *Mother Manual* or something.

"But you already *are* pretty, honey," she said. "You're as cute as you can be. And at school I bet you're—"

I put my hand over my ears. "No. I'm not, Mother! I'm a four-eyed, geeky girl! And I never should have been in this election in the first place. No one in their right mind would ever vote for me."

"That's *not* true, Rosie," she argued back. "I'm sure there are plenty of kids who will—"

I started to cry.

"No, there aren't, Mother! I know better than you do, and there aren't!"

My mother waited a minute. "Please, Rosie. Open up," she said quietly.

Finally, I wiped my eyes with my blanket and I opened my door.

My mother didn't say another word.

We just sat on the edge of my bed. And I let her hug me.

9 LIKE WILDFIRE

The next morning, Neil McNulty saw my note as soon as he pulled out his chair. I was still feeling mixed up about stuff, but I didn't try to stop what was about to happen. I just peeked at Neil through a crack in my three-ring binder and waited.

When he first saw the note, he brushed it onto the floor. I was afraid he might just leave it there. But he must have seen the writing on it, because he leaned over and picked it up again.

He read it. "Whoa!" he hollered.

Then right away, he turned around and tapped Mona Moore on the shoulder. "Get a load of this, Mo!" he said excitedly.

After Mona finished the note, her eyes were practically bulging out of their sockets. She passed it on to Cory Piper. Then Cory passed it to Mallory Fowler. And Mallory passed it to Matthew

Lily. And it just kept going on and on like that, all around the room.

Everywhere, kids were whispering. Finally, Mr. Jolly raised his head and asked what "all the buzzing" was about.

Nobody told him, though. Fourth-graders almost never tell teachers what the buzzing's about.

When the note finally got to Judith Topper, she spun around so fast it made me dizzy. "I bet *you're* the one who wrote this note, Rosie Swanson," she snapped.

Innocent as anything, I stretched my neck and tried to see it. "What note?" I asked.

She threw it on my desk. "This note! You wrote this lie about Alan Allen. You know you did."

I smoothed the paper out in front of me and pretended to read. By now, some of the other kids had turned around and were watching my reaction.

As soon as I was done, I rolled my eyes. "Give me a break, Judith," I said. "Do I really look like the kind of girl who dots my *i*'s with hearts?"

Judith's face turned red with anger. "Liar, liar, pants on fire," she said. Then she started doing the "for shame" sign. That's the one where you brush your pointer finger over your other pointer finger.

I didn't let it bother me, though. Instead, I gave her the "cuckoo" sign and went back to what I was doing.

A few seconds later, a voice came over the intercom.

"MR. JOLLY?"

The voice belonged to Mrs. Trumbull, the grouchy school secretary.

Mr. Jolly looked up from his attendance book. "Yes?"

"MR. JOLLY, COULD YOU PLEASE SEND…"

Mrs. Trumbull paused. Whenever she calls someone to the office, she waits a couple of seconds to make everyone in the room sweat it out.

"…ROSIE SWANSON TO THE OFFICE."

At first, it didn't even register.

Mr. Jolly raised his eyebrows. "Rosie?"

That's when it hit me. Oh my gosh! It was me!

Everybody turned around to look. Judith Topper clapped.

I tried my best to act calm. "Probably just another candidates' meeting," I said as I stood up. But my mouth was so dry my lips stuck together.

I still don't remember walking to the office that morning. But when I finally got there, Mrs. Trumbull pointed her finger at Mr. Shivers' office and said, "They're waiting."

I peeked through the door.

Summer Lynne Jones and Alan Allen were sitting across from Mr. Shivers' desk. I felt myself relax a little. Maybe it really *was* a candidates' meeting.

When I finally got the nerve to go inside, I tried to act as normal as I could.

I waved my fingers at everyone. "Hi, Mr. Shivers. Hi, Summer. Hi, Alan. Hi, Maxie."

Maxie? I thought. What was Maxie doing here?

One thing for sure, he definitely did not look happy. His arms were folded real angry-like, and his cheeks were all sucked into his face.

Normally, I would have sat next to him, but with his face all shrunken in like that, he was scaring me a little.

Before I could sit down, I heard Mrs. Trumbull starting to yell.

"Hey! Put that phone down, young man! Put it down this instant!"

After that, there was some quiet mumbling.

"No, you are *not* having a stroke," she snapped again. "Now go into Mr. Shivers' office right now."

The next thing I knew, Earl Wilber was standing in the doorway. No one falls apart at the principal's office worse than Earl Wilber. His face was pale and sick-looking.

He slipped into the chair next to Maxie and started taking deep breaths. I sat down next to him. Except for his nose whistling, the room was totally quiet.

After making us fidget for a while, Mr. Shivers finally reached into his pocket and pulled out four small yellow notes. He unfolded one of them and began to read:

"Dear Fourth Grade Friend,

Alan Allen stole Rosie Swanson's campaign ideas. Also, he stole a soccer ball from Mort's Sports. Is this really the kind of person you want to elect for president of the fourth grade?

Sincerely yours,

The Committee Who Wants You to Be a Good Voter."

As soon as he finished, Alan Allen exploded out of his chair and pointed at Maxie and Earl and me.

"It was *them,* Mr. Shivers," he said. "They were the ones who passed those notes! Zuckerman is the only kid who I told about the soccer ball thing. And so he told Rosie. And she told Earl. And then the three of them got together and wrote those notes!"

"No, we did *not!*" Maxie yelled back at him. "I've never seen those notes before in my life!"

"Liar!" yelled Alan.

Earl slid down in his seat. "Oh geez, oh geez, oh geez," he muttered nervously.

Mr. Shivers stood up. "Enough!"

Instantly, everyone shut up. Even Earl's nose stopped whistling.

The principal walked around his desk and put Alan Allen back in his chair. Then he stood in front of us for a minute—mostly to show us how big he was, I think—and went back to his seat.

After that, he made his voice so spooky quiet you could hardly hear it. "We do not *scream* in the principal's office, people," he said. "Not *ever.*"

He narrowed his eyes into thin slits. "Got it?"

The five of us nodded as fast as we could.

"Good," said Mr. Shivers. "Now, here's what I'm going to do. I'm going to ask each one of you a very simple question. And all I want is a yes or a no answer. Understand?"

After we nodded again, he swiveled his chair around to face Summer Lynne Jones.

"Okay, Miss Jones. I'm going to ask you first. Did you have anything at all to do with the note I just read?"

"No," said Summer. "I didn't. I promise, Mr. Shivers. I promise, I promise, I prom—"

Mr. Shivers held up his hand to cut her off.

"Good. Fine. Thank you," he said.

Next, he turned to Maxie. "Same question, Mr. Zuckerman. Did you have anything at all to do with the note I—"

"No," interrupted Maxie. "No, no, no, no, no."

When Mr. Shivers got to Earl, his face softened a little. "How 'bout you, Earl? Do you know anything about that note?"

Earl dabbed at the sweat on his face with his shirt sleeve. His voice cracked when he said, "No."

All of sudden, I just couldn't stand it anymore. "I don't understand this, Mr. Shivers," I blurted. "Who cares who wrote the note? Alan's the one who stole the soccer ball, right? Isn't *that* what we should be talking about? I mean, if someone robs a bank and a reporter writes about it, the reporter shouldn't get blamed for spreading the word. It's the crook who should be in trouble."

Alan jumped up again. "But I'm *not* a crook! Just because I took a soccer ball from Mort's Sports Store doesn't make me a crook. I was only in first grade when that happened. That's practically a baby! You can't blame a person for something he did when he was six! And besides, I didn't even get to the car before my dad saw it under my shirt, and he made me take it back."

Alan was so upset he was crying, practically. It kind of surprised me, if you want to know the truth. I just hadn't expected him to almost cry, that's all.

I turned my head and tried not to look at him.

Mr. Shivers narrowed his eyes at me.

"Was it you, Rosie?" he asked at last. "Hmm? Were you the one who wrote the notes?"

By now, I was so mixed up I didn't know what to do. All I'd done was tell the truth. And now *I* was the one in trouble. Since when was being a truthful person such a terrible thing?

Nervously, I pulled at my collar and tried to see the note on the desk. "Well, um, just for the record, I'm not the type of girl who usually dots my *i*'s with hearts."

Mr. Shivers closed his eyes.

"Yes or no?"

Stalling for time, I leaned down and pretended to dust off my shoes.

Alan blew his nose.

Quietly, I said, "Yes."

That afternoon, when I came in from lunch recess, it was written all over the board:

Rosie Swanson is a snitch!

The news spread like wildfire.

10 THE SECOND TUESDAY IN NOVEMBER

Maxie and Earl didn't wait for me after school. I walked home by myself. On the way, three of Alan Allen's friends rode past me on their bikes and shouted, "Yo, snitch! Hi, snitch! How ya doin', snitchy snitch?"

I blinked back the tears. Then I cupped my hands around my mouth. "I know you are, but what am I?"

The boys mimicked me. *"I know you are, but what am I? I know you are, but what am I?"* they said in high, screechy voices.

I stuck out my tongue. Sometimes sticking out your tongue is the only insult you have left.

Face it, Rosie, I said to myself. Your campaign is done for. No one will vote for you now. Not anyone.

I closed my eyes and tried to picture myself

with my bullhorn and golden crown, but nothing happened at all.

As soon as Alan's friends had ridden off, I ran home. It was one of those times when I really needed my mother. I'm not a baby or anything, but sometimes just knowing she's there makes me feel better about stuff. Safer or something, I guess you'd say.

I hurried into the house and slammed the door behind me. "Mom?" I called. "Mom? Are you home?"

"Hi, sweetie," said a voice. It wasn't my mother's voice, though. It belonged to my baby-sitter, Mrs. Rosen from Next Door. That's exactly what she calls herself, too. "Mrs. Rosen from Next Door." When I was little, I used to think it was her name.

"It's Mrs. Rosen from Next Door," she yelled from the kitchen. "I'm in the kitchen, Rosie. How 'bout some Oreos and milk?"

That's mostly what Mrs. Rosen from Next Door does when she baby-sits. She sits in the kitchen, watches the TV on the counter, and eats Oreos.

I like Mrs. Rosen from Next Door. But when the whole world hates your guts, it takes more than a cookie to make it better.

I almost started to cry again. Instead, I ran straight upstairs and called Maxie. I knew he was mad at me. But he was still my friend and I needed him.

Mrs. Zuckerman answered the phone. "It's for you, Max!" she shouted. He must have asked who it was because his mother screamed, "I think it's Rosie!" right in my ear.

After that, I waited and waited, but Maxie never said "Hello." I thought I heard him breathing once. But when I said his name, he didn't answer.

"Maxie? Come on. *Please.* Say something," I said.

I heard a click. Then the dial tone.

That's when I finally started to cry.

The next morning, when I got to Maxie's house, Earl was sitting on the porch step.

"Hi," I said as I walked up.

Earl lowered his head and mumbled, "H'lo." I knew he was still upset about his trip to the principal's office, but at least he was still speaking to me.

Earl kept his head down and stared at his shoes. He untied them, tied them, and untied them again.

After a second, I heard a noise. I looked up. Maxie was standing in his doorway glaring down at me. When he finally came outside, he walked straight down the stairs and kept on going. It was clear that he didn't want to talk to me.

Earl jumped up and followed him. His shoes were still untied but he kept on walking.

At first it almost made me cry again. But pretty soon, I started to get mad. What was wrong with them, anyway? *I* was the one who was in trouble at school, not them. And besides, hadn't I forgiven them when they'd blabbed out all my campaign secrets?

"Hey. Come on, you guys! Why are you acting like this? You're not being very good friends, you know."

Maxie stopped in his tracks and threw his head back. "Ha! That's a good one, isn't it, Earl?" he said sarcastically. "You and I spend the afternoon in the principal's office because of you-know-who, and *we're* the ones who aren't being good friends. Ha!"

He whispered something in Earl's ear.

Earl turned around and cleared his throat. "Maxie says that you're the one who doesn't know anything about friendship, Rosie. You're the one who almost got us blamed for something we didn't do."

I put my hands on my hips. "Okay, fine. I'm sorry. But all I did was tell the truth about Alan. That's all I did. And besides, I'm the one who everybody hates, not you two."

Maxie did another loud "Ha!" and whispered something else.

Earl turned to face me again. "Maxie says if you're the one they hate, then why did he and I get hit with water balloons on our way home from school yesterday?"

Maxie couldn't hold it in anymore. "Yeah! And ask her who crank-called my house last night and wanted to know if the dirty little pipsqueak squealer was home. Go ahead, Earl. Ask her that one!"

Earl took a deep breath. "Maxie would also

like to know who called his house last night and asked if the dirty little pipsqueak—"

He tried to finish, but he started to laugh.

Maxie gave him a shove. "It's not funny, Earl," he growled. "I told Rosie all that stuff about Alan Allen and the soccer ball 'in confidence.' Ask her if she knows what 'in confidence' means. Because for her information, 'in confidence' means that you trust somebody not to tell."

Maxie frowned at me. "You had no right to do that, Rosie! I get picked on enough as it is without having people think I wrote that note. And also, just in case you haven't figured it out yet, you also screwed up your whole election. Who's going to vote for you now? Huh? Who the heck is going to vote for a snitch?"

The way he said "snitch" made me feel dirty, sort of. Like I was a criminal.

"I'm sorry, Max. I'm sorry, I'm sorry," I told him.

My eyes started to fill up again.

When Earl saw what was happening, he ripped off a piece of his lunch sack for me to wipe them with.

After that, all of us started to walk. We didn't talk anymore, though. Not about anything.

When we finally got there, the bell was already ringing. I reached for the door.

Maxie put his hand on my shoulder. "Who knows? Maybe it'll be okay," he said.

"I'm sorry," I said again. "I didn't mean to get you in trouble, Maxie. All I did was—"

Maxie held up his hand. "I know, Rosie. I know," he said. "All you did was tell the truth."

On the morning of the election, the candidates gathered in Mrs. Munson's room before the assembly. Everybody looked really nervous. We were supposed to be reading over our speeches and stuff, but mostly all we could do was fidget around.

Alan Allen asked Mrs. Munson if he could give the first president's speech so he could get it over with. Summer Lynne Jones asked to go last.

I asked to go home.

Mrs. Munson said no.

Finally, we all marched into the media center together. Just like before, the candidates for president were the last to speak. It seemed to take forever before they got to us, too. But when Alan Allen's turn finally came, he stood up slowly and waited for everyone to get totally quiet. Then he walked to the microphone and began.

"My name is Alan Allen," he said. "And I'm running for president of the fourth grade.

"Most of you already know me. I've gone to this school since kindergarten, so I think you know what kind of person I am. I guess if I had to describe myself, I'd say that I'm a good soccer player. And I'd say that I'm honest, too. I don't care what you've heard, either. Because I am."

He glanced over at me, then back again. "There's a rumor going around about how I stole a soccer ball one time," he said. "And I'm not saying it's a lie, okay? Only what you probably don't know is that it happened when I was in first grade. I was only six years old. And even though certain people might not understand this, I did a lot of stuff when I was a little kid that I wouldn't do now.

"Like my mother says I used to scream in restaurants and rub crackers in my hair and junk. And one time when I was in a grocery store, I opened a box of animal crackers, ate a lion, and then put the box back on the shelf. But that doesn't mean I'd do it now. 'Cause that would be stupid. Just like stealing is stupid.

"And so I guess I'd just like to say that if you elect me president of the fourth grade, I promise not to do anything stupid. And I'll be fair. And I'll be honest. And oh yeah...I won't rub crackers in my hair at lunch. Because even though certain people don't understand this, I'm not six years old anymore."

There was lots of clapping when he sat down. It lasted longer than I expected, too. Long enough for Alan to do two extra bows.

By then, my knees were shaking like crazy and I felt weaker than anything. I still don't know how I made it to the microphone. But somehow I did.

Finally, I took a couple of deep breaths and started my speech.

"Hi. My name is Rosie Swanson, and as you probably know, I'm not one of the popular kids. Mostly, I'm just a regular, average girl. But in a way, that's sort of what made my campaign differ-ent. Because you almost never see a regular, average kid running for office. And I don't really get that at all, you know? Because not being popular doesn't mean that you're stupid or anything.

"I mean, personally, I have lots of neat ideas about how to make school a better place. Like I know you've seen my funny posters about the cafeteria food around here. But I have an actual plan about how we can organize a committee to go talk to Mrs. Gumm, the head cafeteria lady. And how we can make lists of all the foods we really hate. And how we can make other lists of all the foods we'd really like to see on the weekly menus and stuff.

"I've had all of these ideas for a long time. But I didn't say anything because I was afraid they would be stolen. That's one thing I've learned about politics. If you have a really good idea, it's okay for somebody else to take it.

"Oh yeah…and there's something else I need to tell you about, too. It's about what happened with Alan Allen and the notes and stuff. I mean, I'm sure you guys know that I wrote those notes about how he stole that soccer ball. And it was wrong of me to do that, I guess. Because I understand that Alan was only six when he took it. And I'm sure that he won't ever steal another soccer ball in his whole entire life, probably."

I paused a second. "But, see, here's the part that's still kind of confusing to me. Because, even back *then*—when I was only six—I never would have stolen that ball. And it just seems like that should count for something, you know? That I've been honest *all* my life. And that I've always tried to obey the rules. So if you vote for me, I swear I'll be the best, most honest fourth-grade president you ever saw. And I'll try really hard to get us better lunches, too. And I'll do other good stuff, too. I mean it. I will."

A lot of kids clapped. Way more than I expected. In fact, I was just about to take bow number two when Summer Lynne Jones pushed past me to get to the microphone.

She didn't look one bit nervous, either. Mostly, she just seemed in a hurry to begin.

"Hi," she said. "My name is Summer Lynne Jones."

She waited until the room was completely quiet. Then she leaned into the microphone.

"I only have two things to say…

"First, I've never stolen anything in my life.

"And second, I'm not a snitch."

She looked around the room and shrugged.

"It's your choice," she said.

Then—without another word—she sat back down.

At the end of the day, Summer Lynne Jones was president of the fourth grade.

11 SOME STUFF I'VE LEARNED...

I'm still not exactly sure what happened that day. I mean, I know that Summer Lynne Jones got the most votes and all. But I'm not positive it's because everyone thought she would make such a great president. After what happened with Alan and me, I just don't think the voters had much choice.

Nic and Vic Timmerman lost, too. So did Roxanne Handleman and Louise the Disease. I saw Louise in the girls' room after school. She was blowing her nose on a paper towel.

Maxie wasn't very sympathetic about my loss. "You did it to yourself, you know," he told me. "You messed up your whole image by writing those tattletale notes."

I tried not to show my disappointment. "Yeah, well, whatever," I said. "It's not the end of the world or anything. I mean, the three of us aren't any worse off than we were before, are we? You're still smart, right? And Earl can still draw. And I still...well, I still..."

"Wear glasses," teased Earl.

I hit him.

One thing I know for sure. Running for president doesn't get a person much respect. Like the other day, the three of us got twirled around on the swings again by those same sixth-grade bullies.

"Wait! Hold it!" I yelled while they were twisting my chain. "Don't you guys even recognize me? I ran for president of the entire fourth grade."

"Whoa, I'm impressed," said one of them. "Aren't you, Frankie? Aren't you impressed?"

After that, they spun me twice as fast as they spun Maxie and Earl.

I got twenty-two votes. Judith Topper told me that. She overheard Mrs. Munson talking about it in the office. Alan Allen got thirty.

"Twenty-two votes was the worst," said Judith. "I guess you know what that makes you. That makes you the big loser...L-O-O-S-E-R."

The girl can't spell worth beans.

The truth is, though, I actually think that

twenty-two votes is pretty darn good. I mean, after everything that happened, I still convinced twenty-one people besides myself that I would make the best president.

I'm almost positive that Norman Beeman was one of them. He came up to me after school and watched me while I buttoned my sweater. Then all of a sudden, he swooped his ball cap off his head and covered his heart with it.

"My sincere condolences," he said. *Condolences* are sort of like heartaches or something, I think.

It was nice. But still, it creeped me out a little.

Another nice thing happened, too. The next day on the playground, two girls from Mrs. Munson's class came up to me and said, "Too bad you lost. We were definitely going to vote for you before that snitch thing."

I'm not sure that they meant it as a compliment, but that's how I took it. 'Cause if two total strangers were going to vote for me, then maybe a lot of other total strangers were going to vote for me, too.

And so this is what I'm thinking. I'm thinking

that maybe one of these days I might try running for class office all over again. 'Cause my grandfather says that when life gives you a kick in the pants, you're supposed to pick yourself up, dust yourself off, and kick it right back again.

And anyhow, I think I've learned some stuff about being a better candidate. I mean, I know I'd do better the next time. I even made a list of things to remember about politics. I call it:

SOME STUFF I'VE LEARNED

ABOUT RUNNING FOR CLASS OFFICE

1. Think of the best campaign ideas you can. If they're not any good, see what your opponents have come up with. (Borrowing ideas is okay in this case.)
2. Be nice to people who make you sick—but not nice enough to make you ashamed of yourself.
3. Smile a lot...but don't give people the creeps.
4. A person is not a crook if he stole something before the age of seven, apparently.
5. No one likes a snitch.

I put the list on my mirror. I look at it every day.

Last night I had a dream about my bullhorn. And my crown.

I woke up smiling.

I think it was a sign.

Maxie's Words

dingle (ding´ gul)—A narrow valley; glen. (p. 29)

fardel (far´ dl)—A bundle; pack; burden. (p. 33)

farkleberry (far´ kul ber e)—A shrub or small tree of
the heath family. (p. 9)

snool (snool)—One who is meanly subservient. (p. 76)

Barbara Park is one of today's funniest, most popular writers for middle-graders. Her novels, which include *Skinnybones, The Kid in the Red Jacket, Rosie Swanson: Fourth-Grade Geek for President,* and *Dear God, Help!!! Love, Earl,* have won just about every award given by children.

She has also created the Junie B. Jones character for the Random House Stepping Stone Books list. Recent books about Junie include *Junie B. Jones Is (almost) a Flower Girl, Junie B. Jones and the Mushy Gushy Valentime,* and *Junie B. Jones Has a Peep in Her Pocket.*

Ms. Park earned a B.S. degree in education at the University of Alabama and lives in Scottsdale, Arizona, with her husband.

If you liked *Rosie Swanson: Fourth-Grade Geek for President,* then don't miss the other two books in the Geek Chronicles trilogy!

Geek Chronicles 1:
Maxie, Rosie, and Earl—Partners in Grime

Meet Maxie, Rosie, and Earl— three kids who unite as they await their doom at the principal's office. Shy Earl is there because he refused to read out loud in class. Nosy Rosie is in trouble because her teacher is sick of her tattling. And then there's Maxie, who finally got tired of being teased and took matters into his own hands. Now they wait like sitting ducks. But no matter what the outcome may be, these three bumbling outlaws have just begun the start of a memorable friendship...

> "Park does it again. Here's a book so funny,
> readers can't help but laugh out loud."
> —*Booklist*

Available wherever books are sold!
ISBN: 0-679-80643-1

Geek Chronicles 3:
Dear God, Help!!! Love, Earl

Wimpy Earl Wilber has just met
death, and his name is Eddie
McFee. Eddie is the meanest,
toughest kid in the fifth grade,
and Earl has to pay him one
dollar a week to keep Eddie
from beating him up. Luckily,
Earl's pals, Rosie the Snoop and
Maxie the Brain, have decided
to help him out. Maxie has a
great plan that should keep
Eddie out of Earl's life for good.
Now all Earl has to do is pretend to be dead...

"Barbara Park is one of the funniest writers
around" (*Booklist*)—and she's got 40
Children's Choice awards to prove it!

Available wherever books are sold!
ISBN: 0-679-85395-2